STOLEN
MAGIC

GAIL CARSON LEVINE

STOLEN
MAGIC

HARPER
An Imprint of HarperCollinsPublishers

Library of Congress Control Number: 2015931902
ISBN 978-0-06-170637-0 (trade bdg.)
ISBN 978-0-06-170638-7 (lib. bdg.)

Typography by Andrea Vandergrift
15 16 17 18 19   PC/RRDH   10 9 8 7 6 5 4 3 2 1

First Edition

To Karen Romano Young
for her thoughtful edits and for staying power!

ACKNOWLEDGMENTS

To Rosemary Brosnan for insight, thoroughness, insistence on excellence

To Renée Cafiero for your care, for what you teach me about the important nitty-gritty, like flapping dependent clauses and the comma splice!

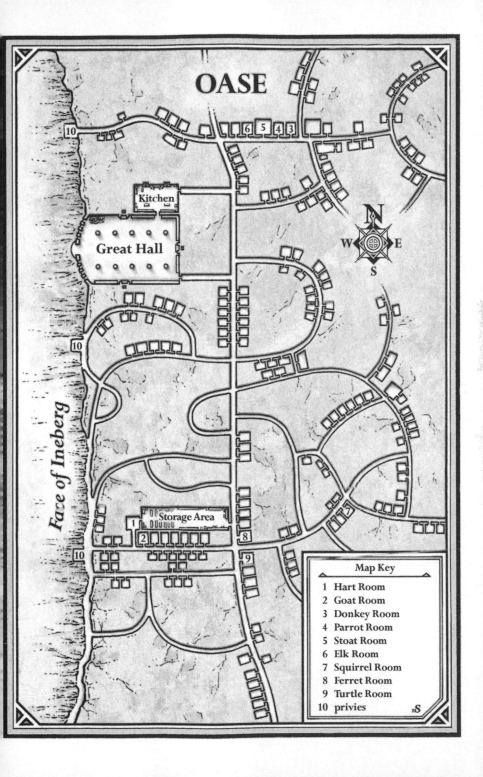

CHAPTER ONE

s if she were narrating a mansioners' play, Elodie spoke across the strait. "And so our heroine"—she blushed at calling herself *heroine*—"young mistress Elodie, returns to Lahnt, the island of her birth. Five weeks earlier, she departed, a humble farmer's daughter, but now, unexpected by all, least expected by herself, she has become—" She broke off as the deck of the cog groaned behind her and the sour odor of rotten eggs reached her nose.

Her traveling companions joined her at the bow railing while the cog rose and fell in moderate swells. On her right, His Lordship, Count Jonty Um, an ogre, who rarely spoke, said nothing. His dog, Nesspa, a tawny, long-haired mountain hound—a big dog for a person but not for an ogre—sat at his feet, panting.

On Elodie's left, her masteress, the dragon Meenore, creator of the foul smell, drawled in ITs nasal voice, "I believe I see a pimple on the horizon, Lodie."

"*E*lodie." She breathed through her mouth. She had come to like ITs stench, but the adjustment always took a few moments.

"Do not correct your elders, *Lodie*." IT used her full name only on grand occasions when she'd won ITs approval. "And certainly not your employer." IT was a detecting dragon, and she ITs assistant.

A winter wind straight from Lahnt attacked the cog. She clutched her cap—newly bought, hardly worn by its former owner, mainland made, pink with red roses—and squinted into the distance. Might that dot be Lahnt? she wondered. Right now at Potluck Farm, smaller than a pinprick in the dot, Mother would be dressing under the coverlet, while Father, already in his tunic and hose, added a log to the fire. His helper, her friend Albin, would be imploring the sun to stop rising and grant him more sleep. It was Albin who'd taught her to mansion—act.

If she were there—if she'd never left home—she'd be laughing at Albin, jumping up for Father's morning hug, eager for Mother's pottage and even for her tart chiding, but dreading another day herding geese.

When she returned, however, she'd have the happiness of home and the joy of the people she loved. The geese

2

would be bearable, since they were no longer her fate.

"What should we know of your native land, Lodie?"

She leaned back against the bulwark railing and addressed ITs ugly face, the long snout covered in brown-and-orange scales and the lipless mouth over which hung two crooked yellow fangs. "Just mountains and farms and tiny villages, Masteress. Few own anything worth caring about if it's lost." IT excelled at finding lost items. "Lahnt has brunkas, though."

"Brunkas . . . Brunkas . . ." ITs smoke rose in puffs. "Brunkas . . . Ah, yes. Not human or fairy or elf. Certainly not dragon or ogre. Residing on the island of Lahnt and nowhere else, and not numerous even there. One lives on every mountain, and one in each village. A bevy dwell together in the north, where the children—"

"Brunkles," Elodie said. "That's what young brunkas are—"

"Neither interrupt nor correct your elders, Lodie. Where the brunkles are born and raised. Brunkas are short creatures even when full-grown, kindly, oddly willing to sacrifice their comfort for others. Calm and rarely rattled. Possessed of sharpened senses: sight, hearing, and smell."

Count Jonty Um boomed—he could speak softer than a boom only with effort—"They can make rainbows, can't they, Elodie?" He always used her full name, and she always had his approval.

She craned her neck up at his pleasant, enormous face. "Most can just flick out little ones, but I'm told High Brunka Marya can send hers across a whole valley."

IT wrinkled ITs eyebrow ridges. "They have their flaws, too, do they not? Good, but faultfinding. Uncompromising."

Elodie rushed to their defense. "They help the deserving!"

"And decide who that is, Lodie."

She shrugged. "Some say they're the best thing about Lahnt."

Others disagreed.

In the afternoon the cog docked in the tiny harbor village of Zee. Elodie couldn't miss the villagers' fright when they saw an ogre and a dragon. Her stomach, though pleased to be on dry land, tightened. Albin, who'd seen the world, wouldn't mind, but her father's teeth chattered at the mere mention of ogres or dragons. Lambs and calves! Mother might run at them with the long rake, as she'd done when a bear had lumbered into their yard. Masteress Meenore cared nothing about the disdain of others, but His Lordship suffered, and Elodie ached in sympathy.

What if her parents were to insist that IT and His Lordship leave and she remain at home?

The three stayed in Zee barely long enough to buy

provisions for the journey and to load two oxcarts, the first with His Lordship's many trunks and Masteress Meenore's hoard (mostly cases of books, although IT couldn't read). Elodie's thin satchel went on top in a blink. The second cart held Masteress Meenore. IT could fly great distances but trudge only short stretches. His Lordship walked next to the first cart, guiding the oxen. Nesspa kept pace at his side.

Elodie drove the second cart. Masteress Meenore rested ITs head next to her on the driver's bench and kept her warm.

Of course they could have flown. Elodie's masteress had carried her on ITs back in the past, and—but for Nesspa—His Lordship could have shifted into a bird. There was no rush, however. The count was traveling for pleasure; Masteress Meenore had come along for pay and curiosity. Both wanted to see the wonders on the way to Elodie's parents' Potluck Farm, where they hoped to spend the winter.

Elodie tightened her jaw. If Mother and Father wouldn't consent to her companions' presence, she'd leave with them, for the excellent reason that Masteress Meenore provided her livelihood—her fascinating livelihood.

An hour outside Zee they camped for the night. The journey north would take two weeks if the weather favored them. November could be mild or harsh, and few traveled between October and April. Lahnt ran southwest to northeast, a hundred fifty miles long, the whole of it a chain of seven mountains, as close together as teeth in a wolf's jaw. The one major river, the Fluce, wound through the valleys. The one major road kept to the midslopes, above the spring floods. The going was rough even when the sun shone, as it did the next morning when they set out in earnest.

Natural marvels surrounded them: enormous sky, spiky peaks, sheep and goats dotting the mountainsides, purple-and-white toad lilies that lined the road and bloomed in Lahnt even through light snow, blue waters of the strait to the southeast, and green waves of the ocean to the west, both visible on a clear day. But these sights were all too familiar to a farmer's daughter who hated farming.

As they rounded Bisselberg, the lowest mountain in the range, IT surprised Elodie, who had never heard IT sing before, with a ditty:

> "There once was a dragon called Larragon,
> who wore neither robe nor cardigan
> yet was still fashion's true paragon
> with scales that sparkled like platinum
> as ITs crimson flame flared and carried on."

IT switched register from line to line, soprano to bass and back, confounding Elodie yet again as to ITs gender.

Someday, she swore silently, I will find out.

"Travel brings out the minstrel in me, Lodie. Perhaps I will sing again and torment you anew with curiosity." IT laughed, sounding like a donkey holding its nose: *Enh enh enh.*

Later, while they shared their midday meal, IT asked, "What are the mountains called?"

Elodie paused with a meat pasty—a small meat pie—halfway to her lips and rattled them off: "South to north: Bisselberg, Ineberg, Svye, Zertrum, Navon, Dair, Letster."

"Did you learn the names charmingly as a babe at your mother's side, Lodie?"

She swallowed a morsel of pasty. "I suppose. 'Bear Is So Zany, No Dogs Lie.'"

His Lordship murmured loudly, "Nesspa never lies," and scratched the dog behind his ears.

"Ah. A memory device derived from the first letter of each mountain. Bisselberg, Ineberg, Svye, Zertrum, Navon, Dair, Letster. Beautiful Island's Seven Zeniths Never Disappoint Lahnters. Mine is better."

How clever IT is, Elodie thought proudly. "Mine is shorter and easier to recall."

"You will remember mine forever. Will we soon approach any Lahnt landmarks?"

"We aren't far from the Oase, where thousands of relics of Lahnt and brunka history are kept. It's on Ineberg, the next mountain. High Brunka Marya, the Ineberg brunka, lives there with her bees—her helpers."

"Insects?"

"Bees are people, Your Lordship. You might think they're servants, but they're more than that. The Oase is close to the road. We could stop"—she mansioned the longing out of her voice—"if you're interested." The Oase held the Replica, Lahnt's most important wonder. Every Lahnter wanted to see it at least once, and she never had.

"Does the high brunka like ogres?"

"She's probably never met any. But brunkas are friendly."

Count Jonty Um said nothing for a full five minutes, then, "Perhaps we can come back before we leave Lahnt."

A lump of sympathy rose in Elodie's throat. His Lordship had reason to be shy. She swallowed her disappointment and the lump. "Of course." With luck they'd meet a brunka on the road, and with more luck, the brunka wouldn't greet an ogre with fright and loathing. Then the count might really want to come back.

At night, after the evening meal, they slept under bright stars, Elodie rolled up in her cloak, His Lordship rolled up in his, Nesspa curled in the crook of his knees, the three of them close enough to Masteress Meenore to enjoy ITs warmth.

A wet dawn woke them. They crossed the valley between Bisselberg and Ineberg in a steady rain. As the carts climbed the lower slopes of Ineberg, the downpour turned to snow. His Lordship lifted Nesspa into his cart. IT spread a wing protectively over Elodie, whose cloak steamed dry in a trice. While the landscape turned the page from fall to winter, she sat, munching on a raisin roll, in an alcove of summer.

The snow thickened. Occasionally they passed a path, which would be the route up the mountain to a farm cottage or down to the river.

By evening, they were in a blizzard. Snow invaded Elodie's haven under Masteress Meenore's wing.

The road vanished. Elodie's oxen halted. She couldn't see the cart ahead—or her hand an inch from her eyes. Snow surrounded them, wove them into a frigid cocoon. She wondered how His Lordship, Nesspa, and the oxen could draw air to breathe.

Where was His Lordship? Were his oxen still lumbering on?

People and beasts died regularly in blizzards on Lahnt, although she was in no danger. Nor was His Lordship—if he could make his way back to them. Masteress Meenore would keep them both warm, but she doubted IT had heat enough to prevent the oxen from freezing to death.

Where was His Lordship?

CHAPTER TWO

T broke into song, bellowing loud enough to almost drown out the howling wind.

"There once was a dragon called Kacial
who stayed in when the day was glacial.
Because ITs flame would snuff out
from any snow on ITs snout,
IT remained in ITs lair palatial."

His Lordship's form took shape out of a white world. He deposited Nesspa in the cart with Masteress Meenore and shouted into ITs earhole. Elodie could hear him only faintly: "I'll bring the oxen past you and round and round. If you warm them, and they keep moving, one or two may live."

One or two? Out of eight!

She couldn't hear ITs answer, but she did hear IT sing again.

"There once was a dragon named Gizzard,
who, when caught in a blizzard,
danced with a spin and a hop,
a heated and happy dragon gavotte
that would have astonished a wizard."

The oxen filed by under ITs outstretched wing while IT continued to bawl out verses about dragons named this and that. The evening dragged on.

A new shape, no bigger than Elodie, arrived just outside the scope of ITs wing. It brushed snow off itself and became a small woman, waving a hand in front of her nose. Even in a blizzard, IT stank.

Elodie blinked. Not a small woman. A brunka!

Lambs and calves! High Brunka Marya?

Elodie formed an impression of a bulbous nose and intent eyes. The brunka wasn't smiling, though brunkas almost always smiled. But this was a blizzard, and she was encountering an ogre and a dragon.

She spoke words that vanished into the wind.

IT roared, "I am gratified you liked my warbling enough to come. Can you conduct us to safety?"

Her masteress had sung to bring help? Elodie shook her head in admiration.

The brunka nodded and made a flinging gesture back in the direction they'd come. Elodie gasped. A rainbow flowed from her finger. The snow, rather than hiding the rainbow, picked up its colors. Snowflakes sparkled like tiny rubies, emeralds, and sapphires. High Brunka Marya—she could be none other—started away under the rainbow, leaning into the wind, struggling through the drifts.

Elodie clasped her hands in delight. Thank you, blizzard. They were going to the Oase after all. The oxen would live, and she'd see the Replica.

The three abandoned the carts. By rainbow glow, Elodie saw His Lordship go by with Nesspa in his arms (licking his face), driving the oxen ahead of them. Elodie set out even with ITs neck but fell back to next to ITs belly and then ITs tail, fighting the wind through snow that mounded, here and there, to her waist.

Masteress Meenore lowered ITself and rolled onto ITs side. "Climb on, Lodie. You are delaying me."

She did. In the past she'd been on ITs back only when IT flew. Now she slipped from side to side on wet scales as IT lumbered along under the rainbow, which arched only a few inches over her head. She tugged off a glove and thrust her hand into the miracle—and yanked it out instantly. Her hand tingled with pins and needles as if it had awakened from a month's sleep.

IT wreathed around ITs head to face her and moralize louder than the blizzard, "Pain, Lodie, is the deserved consequences of a rash act."

Worth it! she thought. She rubbed her hand until the stinging finally stopped and feeling returned. Then she hunched down to get the most of ITs heat, contenting herself with looking up at the rainbow.

They had been struggling downhill, but now they began to climb, and Elodie had to hug ITs neck to keep from sliding off. She cried, "I don't mean to be impertinent," and dimly heard ITs answer, "I did not suspect impertinence . . . until you apologized." *Enh enh enh.*

As the way became steeper, she could think of nothing but hanging on. If she fell off, she'd be lost in one minute and frozen in the next.

At last ITs back leveled. Elodie heard wood groaning, then horses whinnying and donkeys braying. Probably happy braying, because beasts loved His Lordship. They seemed to know he could become one of them. The only exception was cats, who wanted him to shape-shift into a mouse so they could eat him.

Masteress Meenore progressed through a wide door into a large wooden stable dimly lit by a row of coal braziers that ran down the middle, intended to keep the animals from freezing. His Lordship pushed the big door closed, then set Nesspa down.

They were in an open area before the beasts' stalls began. IT lowered ITself to ITs belly, and Elodie slid off. The dog trotted to the stalls, sniffing.

"High Brunka Marya," IT said, "you have succored us. May we return the favor? Your trouble is grave indeed."

CHAPTER THREE

hat trouble could befall a brunka, unless it was trouble for Lahnt? Despite ITs warmth, Elodie felt a chill.

She saw the high brunka better in here: plump, her mother's age, more or less, with a square face, ruddy cheeks, and thick lips that still failed to smile. Below her blue wool cap, her graying brown hair fell to her shoulders in waves. If she had been taller, she'd have been unremarkable: her face as ordinary as a bowl of porridge, her plumpness as kindly as a soft bed. She curtsied to the three of them —a quick, efficient gesture.

Elodie curtsied back, the elaborate court curtsy that Albin had taught her as part of her mansioner training. IT performed ITs usual masculine bow followed by a feminine curtsy. His Lordship must have calculated their relative rank, count to a high brunka. From the midst of the oxen he bowed deeply. Elodie had seen mere head nods from him; this was An Acknowledgment.

"Is someone sick?" Elodie hoped that was all it was.

High Brunka Marya smiled a thin smile. "A barber-surgeon is visiting, lamb." Her voice, though soft as moss, carried. "Except for a toothache, we're as healthy as fleas."

Elodie heard a distinct *tsk* from her masteress, who hated dirt and despised vermin.

"I'm delighted to welcome you to the Oase." The high brunka corrected herself: "To the stable of the Oase. I regret our doorway to the Oase itself is too narrow to admit some of you. Honored guests, I hope we can be hospitable anyway. Strangers rarely visit us."

Ah. Elodie deduced, as IT had taught her, that High Brunka Marya didn't realize she was a Lahnter. She'd been misled by Elodie's mainland cap, her cloak with the flowing sleeves, and her pointy-toed mainland shoes.

High Brunka Marya added, "And nothing is amiss, Masteress. We're right as a good harvest."

She didn't meet ITs eyes, often a sign of a lie, but perhaps not now. ITs flat emerald green eyes were terrifying until you came to know ITs crabby, benevolent nature.

If Masteress Meenore believes something is wrong, Elodie thought, then something is. She detected no vestige of calm in the high brunka, although brunkas were usually

16

placid. Even in the presence of a dragon and an ogre there should have been a little serenity, since the dragon wasn't flaming and the ogre wasn't drooling or eating one of the oxen. In fact, His Lordship was stroking the head of an ox and leading him gently into a stall.

"Begging your pardon, perhaps we can help." Inspired, Elodie proclaimed, as IT had hired her to do, "This evening, in the stable of the Oase and only in the stable of the Oase, the Great, the Unfathomable, the Brilliant Masteress Meenore is available to solve riddles, find lost objects and lost people, and answer the unanswerable. . . ."

Masteress Meenore's smoke rose in white spirals, signifying dragon joy. High Brunka Marya's eyes were amused.

Heartened, Elodie continued, "Three tins for a riddle solved, fifteen tins for a lost object found, three coppers for a lost person found. The fee for answering the unanswerable will be negotiated. During said negotiations or in any discussions with Masteress Meenore, speak to IT with respect."

"Thank you, Elodie."

She grinned in triumph. Her full name!

"The sums cited by—"

"Pardon me, Masteress." Wearing a puzzled frown, High Brunka Marya turned back to Elodie. "Elodie is as Lahnt a name as sheep on a mountain."

Elodie saw no reason to lie, and ITs expression was unreadable. "I'm from Dair Mountain."

She expected a broader smile and a more genuine welcome, but the high brunka's frown deepened.

"Madam," IT said, "you are every moment confirming my conjecture. You recognized Elodie's name, and your unease increased." IT held up a claw because the high brunka began to protest. "There is trouble of a certainty. As Lodie proclaimed, I am brilliant. You believe we are connected to the trouble."

His Lordship left the oxen in four steps. "Is Elodie in danger, Meenore?"

"We may all be at risk. I require information to evaluate, but this brunka has not obliged us. Perhaps we can deduce on our own. Lo—"

"How do you know something is wrong?"

"An admission. Lodie, how did I conclude some calamity had befallen the Oase or the high brunka?"

Elodie felt the familiar pressure of her brain being squeezed. "Er . . . Masteress, you sang so that someone might hear us. Er . . . you knew brunkas have especially sharp ears. And a brunka came. Wasn't that what you expected?" Her coming couldn't mean anything! "Er . . . um . . ."

"You disappoint me. Your Lordship, if someone unknown arrived outside your castle in a blizzard, would you go yourself to see who it was?"

"Yes. A servant might freeze. I could always—"

"Oh!" Elodie had figured it out. "Pardon, Your Lordship. A nobleman less sweet-natured than Count Jonty Um would send a servant. High Brunka, why didn't you send a few of your bees?"

IT didn't give the high brunka time to answer. "Good, Elodie. Why do you think—"

"Masteress . . ."

"You know I do not relish interruptions, Lodie. What is it?"

She approached IT and stood on tiptoe.

IT lowered ITs head.

She whispered into ITs earhole. "The high brunka looks as if . . ." Midsentence she remembered brunka hearing. Feeling foolish, she finished without whispering. "She needs to sit."

"Excellent observation. We do not want our informant to swoon."

High Brunka Marya's face was pale, and she stood on spread feet for balance. "Lamb, you'll find a stack of stools at the end of the stalls."

Elodie hurried through the stable, which held the hired oxen as well as six horses and seven donkeys. She wondered if all these beasts belonged here or if the Oase had guests.

"Bring a stool for yourself, Lodie. Your Lordship, perhaps you can procure a seat that—"

"I'll stand."

Elodie returned with two stools. The high brunka sat on one a few yards from ITs head. Elodie placed her own stool so that the four of them formed a rough diamond. She faced Count Jonty Um's legs, and Masteress Meenore opposed the high brunka.

"Now. To continue. Lodie, why do you think High Brunka Marya came herself?"

"Um . . . because she was expecting someone and she didn't want anyone to know?"

"Think, Lodie! Not unless she expected a singing dragon. She heard my song."

Elodie pressed her hands together. "Er . . . um . . ." An idea came. She tested it and couldn't find anything wrong with it. "Because she hoped we could help her and she didn't want anyone else to know."

"A reasonable inference. She certainly prefers to keep our arrival to herself. There is another possibility as well. She does not anticipate help from us. Rather—"

His Lordship interrupted. "She thinks we're part of whatever is wrong." Unspoken, hanging in the air: No one trusts an ogre.

Elodie's mind raced straight to the worst possible calamity. "High Brunka Marya, has the Replica been stolen?"

"No. Certainly not." The high brunka avoided Elodie's eyes. Her hand went to straighten her cap, and for a moment—a blink—her face became a mask of distress before she recaptured her thin smile.

The mansioner in Elodie recognized the lie. "Lambs and calves! Someone *did* take the Replica. Masteress, this is terrible!" She held her head as if it might fly apart. "If the Replica isn't found, Zertrum Mountain will explode."

CHAPTER FOUR

"Are your parents and Albin at risk, Elodie?"

How kind His Lordship was, to think of them, and to crouch so that his face was level with hers. Her masteress looked merely curious.

She said, "They're safe. Thank you. Navon Mountain stands between our Potluck Farm and Zertrum. But many families live on Zertrum."

"Excellent deducing, Elodie," IT said, "and whatever else you did to root out the truth. Pray, what is this Replica a replica of? And how will its theft cause a mountain to spew?"

Elodie hardly heard. Was a bee the thief? How long had the Replica been gone?

"Lodie, I am waiting." IT shifted ITs gaze to High Brunka Marya. "Madam, no doubt you have more information than Lodie, but I cannot trust you to be honest."

Elodie answered in a rush. "It's a sculpture of the island. I've never seen it, but I've heard it's not much longer than my hand and even narrower. It's heavy because it's made of gold and dotted with jewels. Harald, the first brunka to set foot on Lahnt, who knew a few spells, had it made along with a marble stand to hold it. He put an enchantment on both. When he and his companions came to Lahnt three hundred years ago, Zertrum—that's the middle mountain, the only one with a volcano—had just spewed. He fell in love with Lahnt as soon as he saw it, so he—"

"Is this the case, Madam? It is more than legend? As long as this Replica remains on its stand, the volcano is quiet? Or must the pedestal be taken as well?"

High Brunka Marya shook her head. "Only the Replica, Masteress. It can be taken off briefly to show people. However, the two must not be separated for long. It was stolen—just once, thirty years ago—but we got it back the next day. On the first day, the day of the theft, Zertrum may have rumbled, but so softly no one could tell. A little more on the second day. There were two brunkas on the mountain then, and they felt and heard it. When we placed the Replica back on its pedestal, the mountain quieted."

Masteress Meenore blew a puff of white smoke. "For how long will the protection dwindle before it vanishes entirely?"

Elodie jumped in. "Brunka Harald extended the protection as long as he could, but even he didn't know how long it might last. He thought three days at the most, and near the end it will be very bad—awful." She quoted Brunka Harald: "'The volcano will light the darkness.'"

"That's right, lamb," High Brunka Marya said. "Harald wished he could have sealed the volcano forever without a replica and without danger to anyone, but he didn't know any spells that were powerful enough." She shook her head sadly. "He was just a brunka who had memorized a few enchantments."

"Masteress"—Elodie balled her gloves in her hand—"my mother says the explosion will be the worst ever because the mountain has been quiet for so long."

"Irrelevant, Lodie. Alas, you mistakenly recited my rates for when I am at home in Two Castles. Elsewhere, High Brunka Marya, my costs and my inconvenience are greater. For finding this—"

High Brunka Marya pointed at the oxen and burst out, "Are they ogres, too?"

"I'm the only ogre." His Lordship's voice sounded pained.

Elodie's throat tightened in sympathy.

"His Lordship may be lying, Madam." ITs smoke tinted red with irritation. "All the oxen may be ogres, and their fleas may be ogres, too. You may be harboring a hundred

24

ogres. How fortunate for you if you are. A flock of ogres to shape-shift into birds and fly to Zertrum Mountain and give the alarm. Many ogres to help people off the mountain. More ogres to transform into herding dogs to bring the sheep and goats and geese to safety."

The high brunka looked up at the ceiling, seeming to calculate. "Are they, Masteress?"

"No." *Enh enh enh.* "But His Lordship may be kind enough to fly and warn the mountainside. I could do it, but I will be otherwise engaged."

"Would you, er, Your Lordship?"

Count Jonty Um favored High Brunka Marya with his smile. Elodie's shoulders relaxed. At the least, the high brunka would see his beautiful flat—not pointy—white teeth. And she couldn't miss the sweetness of his smile, the blaze of his goodness gleaming through.

High Brunka Marya blushed, which IT was unable to resist commenting on. "Madam, you do well to regret your defamatory assumptions about our friend."

"I'll fly as a Lepai yellow-feathered swift for speed," (Lepai was the kingdom Lahnt belonged to.) "While Meenore and Elodie are seeking the Replica, will Nesspa be looked after?"

"Of course," the high brunka said.

"Tell me where to go."

She gave him directions to Zertrum Mountain. "The

peak looks like the gaping mouth of a fish. The brunka house, which is made of stone blocks with a slate roof, is on the north slope. You'll know it by the two chimneys."

Poor farm cottages like Elodie's parents' had thatched roofs and only one chimney.

"A stable is attached as well. The brunka who lives there with four bees is Arnulf." She opened her cloak—green wool like her cap, tight weave, excellent quality, though not as rich as His Lordship's—to get at her purse.

"Don't pay me!" Count Jonty Um boomed, sounding loudly horrified.

"If you show this"—she pulled out a gold medal on a brass chain. Stamped into the medal was an image of High Brunka Marya's face—"Arnulf will believe you."

"Wind it around my neck."

The high brunka looked confused. The chain was much too short.

"The bird's neck," Elodie explained. "Your Lordship, can you fly in snow?"

They waited. He seemed to be consulting a bird who lived inside him. Finally he nodded. "When it's just snow, not a blizzard."

"Madam, we still have not resolved the matter of my fee for finding your Replica."

"Masteress!" Saving lives should be free!

"Lodie, do not interfere." ITs smoke reddened. "His

26

Lordship will warn your brunka and will not accept payment. I lack his kind nature. I suppose you would like me to identify the thief as well."

"Masteress . . ." High Brunka Marya tilted her head to look at IT. The worry lines smoothed out, and her face wore the usual calm brunka expression. She smiled the contented brunka smile.

IT coughed at the back of ITs throat. Coming from anyone else, Elodie would have thought the cough an uneasy sound. Folks usually felt uncomfortable under the scrutiny of that serene brunka gaze. But did IT?

"You suspect us," IT said, "as well you may. You should trust no one. People are a perfidious lot. But especially do not trust now."

IT was babbling! The high brunka had unnerved IT!

"Still, if my assistant and—"

"Your assistant? His Lordship?"

"Lodie is my assistant."

She felt a burst of satisfaction.

"I see." But the high brunka sounded as if she didn't.

"If we put ourselves out, we will expect more than a mere fifteen tin coins."

Elodie bit her cheek. How could IT haggle over this?

His Lordship took one step to the door, opened it, and looked out, his broad back to the others. "I'll watch the snow. When the blizzard subsides, I'll shape-shift."

Talk of money was beneath a count.

"Masteress," High Brunka Marya said, "you're as clever as a ratcatcher. If you tell me now where the Replica is and who took it, I'll give you three gold coins, and you, His Lordship, and Elodie won't be imprisoned."

Oh no! Elodie struggled to think of something that would prove their innocence.

"Madam, your suspicions are absurd."

High Brunka Marya raised her eyebrows, still smiling.

"As soon as the blizzard retreats, nothing can stop a shape-shifting ogre from entering your Oase."

The High Brunka's smile faded.

"Mice find their way in when the weather turns cold, do they not? He can become a creature much smaller than a mouse. He can gain admission on your person as a louse."

Enh enh enh.

His Lordship turned his head. "Meenore—"

"Permit me to conduct this conversation, Your Lordship. Once inside, he becomes himself again, crouching if he must. You can imagine the rest: the thief fetches the Replica. No one dares interfere because of an ogre's hulking presence."

Count Jonty Um nodded. "I could do all that. Hypothetically."

Elodie smiled at him for understanding. He winked, a slow, effortful wink.

Masteress Meenore went on. "His Lordship tears the door off its hinges and enlarges your entry. We fly away with Lodie and the thief on my back and His Lordship as the Lepai yellow-feathered swift. Lodie holds the Replica in her lap."

The high brunka's eyes went to Elodie, who mansioned her face to show nothing.

"High Brunka, if we are in league with the thief, you cannot stop us. In the event that we are not, you may as well engage us. If we find the Replica, a mountain will be saved. If we fail, then the villain is smarter than I . . ."

. . . Smarter than both of us, Elodie thought.

". . . which I doubt."

The high brunka bent over so her head was in her lap, a pathetic pose. A tiny rainbow flickered from her right hand.

Was she ill?

"The snow is dwindling," His Lordship reported.

A minute passed in silence. Elodie wanted to pat the high brunka's shoulder.

ITs smoke tinted faintly gray, meaning IT was faintly sad. Sympathy for the high brunka? Elodie wondered. Or for the people on the mountain that might explode?

High Brunka Marya sat up, serenity in place again. "We'll pay whatever you believe reasonable. I trust your fairness."

The corners of ITs mouth turned up.

Greedy dragon! Elodie thought.

Sometimes IT deduced her thoughts. "Self-interest is not precisely greed, Lodie. Self-interest is reasonable. Greed exceeds the bounds of reason."

"I can leave now." His Lordship knelt by Nesspa and rubbed his neck. "Be good, Nesspie. I'll be back soon." He stood and began to raise his arms.

"Wait!"

Masteress Meenore had stopped His Lordship in time. He lowered his arms.

"Upon your arrival, ask the brunka and his bees if they know of anyone who might be angry at them, exceedingly angry, or angry at anyone else on the mountain, or angry at the mountain itself, although they may consider that question odd. Ask also if anyone has recently left Zertrum."

"Ask . . ." Elodie paused, not liking to offend the high brunka, but this wasn't a time to worry about that. "Ask if the brunkas refused aid to anyone recently."

"We never deny help lightly, lamb."

"Excellent, Elodie. Your Lordship, make them answer you."

Count Jonty Um's expression darkened. Elodie knew he hated to be feared, and now he was being told to take advantage of the terror.

Masteress Meenore knew, too. "You are a count—nobility. Use that if you can. But if you must, frighten them. You may save lives."

The high brunka said, "How soon will you be there?"

"Before dawn."

"Will you stay to help people off the mountain? Most folks live in the valley or on the lower slopes, but several families built their cottages high, to be with their flocks." The high brunka clasped her hands in supplication. "Please help them."

"You must not. You may be tempted by your unaccountably kind nature and by the direness of people's need. Resist! I require the answers to my questions if my inquiry is to succeed."

His Lordship raised his arms.

Elodie braced herself. She hated the shifts because His Lordship's face bore such a look of agony. "High Brunka, it may not hurt as much as it seems to. He doesn't say."

"Thank you for telling me, lamb."

His mouth opened in a silent scream; his eyes became slits; his nose wrinkled; his nostrils flared. His body vibrated, became a shrinking blur overwhelmed by his blue cloak and blue cap. His silver pendant on its golden chain slid off the pile of apparel. The ogre seemed to have disappeared.

High Brunka Marya breathed, "Where . . ."

The mound shook, jounced, bounced. Elodie pulled away the yards of cloth to reveal a yellow bird ruffling his feathers. Elodie saw His Lordship's intelligence shining out of his deeply set eyes.

"Why doesn't he go?" High Brunka Marya said.

Elodie remembered first. "He's waiting for you to wind your medal around his neck."

"Ah, yes." She did so, and the swift tolerated her hands. She finished and stood.

Elodie, who hadn't stopped watching her friend, saw the thought fade from the bird's eyes.

Was he frightened to find himself in a stable, so close to a human, a dragon, a brunka?

He cheeped a high, whistling chirp and flew out into the night.

CHAPTER FIVE

he swift circled the stable once and flew north, his being almost overcome by the burdens the ogre had placed on him: a feeling, two images, and two memories. The feeling: urgency. The images: a volcanic mountain peak that looked like a gaping fish and a building with two chimneys and an attached stable. The memories: a long-haired dog and a girl with big eyes and a wide, expressive mouth.

The wind had died to a bare breeze. The snowflakes were shimmering sparkles. In his heart, urgency paired with the joy of flight.

CHAPTER SIX

lodie missed her friend instantly. With careful fingers, she brushed hay off his beautiful cloak. Fly safely. Hurry back.

"Madam, a few questions before you and Elodie leave me."

Leave IT? Of course, for the Oase. She was no use out here.

"When was the Replica stolen?" IT asked.

"I'm not sure. Within the last three days, certainly."

Three *days*? Zertrum might already be about to spew! Lambs and calves! IT should have asked this before His Lordship left! Elodie squeezed his cloak, which filled her arms. What had they sent him into?

"Since then, has anyone departed the Oase?" IT asked.

"No one. I discovered the theft late this afternoon after

the storm began. We have guests, which we rarely do this time of year—"

"Mmm."

ITs *Mmm* always meant something. Elodie felt sure this one meant that these guests might have come in order to commit the theft.

"Poor Master Robbie—he's a pup, as young as this lamb—grew bored because of the snow and being confined indoors. He asked to see the Replica again." She added, "He saw it for the first time right after he arrived."

Elodie decided Master Robbie was a boy, not a puppy. Had he really made his request out of boredom? She felt ITs eyes on her. They exchanged glances. Maybe the boy knew it was gone. She wondered why he was *poor* Master Robbie.

To the left of the stable door stood a rough cupboard, where she thought she might stow Count Jonty Um's clothing. She went to it and lifted the wooden latch. What if the thief had hidden the Replica here, a reasonable spot for an escape on horseback?

But the shelves seemed empty. She used her own cloak to wipe away dust on a middle shelf and placed His Lordship's cloak there, then returned to the heap on the floor for the rest of his things. His boots she placed below the lowest shelf. His silver pendant, which was very valuable, she pushed under his cloak toward the back of the cupboard.

High Brunka Marya was still explaining. "When I went to fetch the Replica, it wasn't there." She stood and paced. "I looked in other places, thinking I might have been absentminded when I put it away." She stopped. "But I wouldn't have been, not with the Replica. I'd never set it down anywhere except on its pedestal."

"Did you raise the alarm?"

She shook her head. "I gave Master Robbie other relics to look at, Masteress. I said I was too tired to fetch it just then and promised to bring it in the morning. He was content."

Elodie's and her masteress's eyes met again. She felt a flash of happiness that they were thinking alike, that the boy's contentment might have been a ruse.

"High Brunka?" Elodie returned to her stool. "Er . . ." She felt shy, questioning a brunka. "Er . . . who else was there when Master Robbie asked for the Replica again, and who was there when you brought him the other relics?"

"When the pup asked, we were gathered around the big fireplace, all the guests and Ursa-bee. When I returned, our cook, Ludda-bee, had come to announce what she was serving for the evening meal, so she was there, too."

If the thief was among them, he or she knew that the theft had been discovered.

"What did you do next?" Masteress Meenore scratched under ITs jaw.

"I went to my chamber to think." The mask of distress covered her face again. Her eyes were tormented. "I knew I had to tell everyone, but I wanted to organize my ideas, which were as scattered as the stars. Then you sang, Masteress, and I came. The guarding bees were dozing at their posts. My movements are almost silent, so they didn't waken."

IT shook ITs big head. "Guards are permitted to sleep?"

"They'd have heard anyone but a brunka."

IT let that stand. "Might the thief escape in your absence, Madam, now that the blizzard has ended?"

"He wouldn't get far on foot in this snow. If he wanted a horse, he'd have to come here."

"He *or she* wouldn't get far. If he *or she* wanted . . . Lodie, can you forgo sleep tonight?"

She nodded. She'd done so before for IT.

"High Brunka, can you show Lodie in secret where the Replica had been kept?"

High Brunka Marya said that almost everyone would be asleep. "The bees who guard the Replica will be awake, but they know where it's kept anyway."

ITs smoke shaded pink. "Mmm," IT said coldly.

She raised her chin and stepped back. "I have no secrets from my bees after they've been with me for three years."

Elodie heard ITs *Fool!* hang in the air unspoken. The high brunka blushed.

"After you have shown Lodie the Replica's hiding place, you must awaken everyone and inform them of the theft. There is not a moment to lose. The snow has lessened. The thief may be contemplating his or her escape. How awkward these he-she and his-her locutions are. How much more efficient to be an IT." *Enh enh enh.*

Elodie stiffened. How could IT laugh now?

"Lodie, if I cannot hold myself apart from events, I will never see them whole. You must cultivate this quality in yourself, which will be essential when the high brunka reveals the theft. No telltale sign in her audience may go unnoticed by you: no blush, no shudder, no sigh, no odor of distress. You must have the heightened senses of a brunka and the perspicacity of a detecting dragon."

What if I miss something, Elodie thought, and it's the most important clue? "Masteress, you should be there."

"Alas, the fear and awe that I inspire would call forth trembling and stares. Even I could not discern which were due to guilt and which to my presence. Better by far that you be the only witness."

She nodded, but she wished that a mountain and His Lordship weren't at stake.

"*Feeling*—whatever you may feel—may not be allowed in. Madam, do not tell anyone that the girl is in my employ. She is a mere child I am returning to her home out of the goodness of a dragon's heart." *Enh enh enh.*

"A half-truth is as false as a whole lie," the high brunka said promptly, as if the words had been waiting on her lips.

ITs smoke purpled. "An exploding volcano will be one complete truth, Madam, and your failure to prevent it will be another."

The high brunka sank onto her stool and spoke to her hands in her lap. A pale rainbow unfurled, then faded. "As you wish, Masteress. I'll lie and try to be convincing."

"Excellent." IT asked and was told that the Oase had a great hall, a large room. "Keep everyone there except for your most trusted bees, those who have been with you at least *seven* years. They may begin a search of the Oase. Have them search in pairs. Better yet, see that they do everything in pairs, and change the pairings often."

Oh! Elodie thought, dismayed. She'd heard that the Oase tunneled into the mountain, spidering into a vast warren of corridors and rooms. How could they hope to find anything as small as the Replica?

"A bee would never take the Replica."

ITs tail twitched. "Madam, that is the assertion of an imbecile. Look at me."

Elodie thought she would shrivel up if IT ever used that tone with her.

High Brunka Marya met ITs eyes. "Brunkas trust hearts and judge acts. That may make us imbeciles to you."

"Just so. Dragons rarely trust."

They dropped their eyes at the same time. IT continued, "Your bees know where the Replica was kept, which almost certainly caused the mischief. A bee was indiscreet, or a bee is the thief."

"I'll do what you suggest."

"As my agent, Elodie will hold you to your promise."

She'd have to mansion an imperious self for that.

ITs smoke whitened. "In the morning, expect me at the Oase entry, ready to interrogate each guest and each bee. Instruct those you can instruct to answer me truthfully. The thief will certainly lie. If everyone else is honest, I may catch an inconsistency."

"Come, lamb." The high brunka stood.

"Go!" IT said.

Elodie wrapped her cloak around herself.

"Wait, Lodie! In the Oase, proceed as if Zertrum were safe for a century. If you rush, you will bungle. You will meet bees and guests and will need to take their measure. I will want your opinion."

"Masteress! There isn't time."

"Mansion that there is. And take care and more care and care again. A thief who would make a mountain explode will not mind destroying *you*."

"I'll keep her safe."

"You let your most important possession be taken."

"I'll be careful, Masteress."

"See that you are. And keep your penetrating mind a secret, Lodie. The appearance of a slow wit . . ."

Elodie hardly heard the end of the sentence. Had IT truly called her clever? If I had dragon smoke, she thought, it would be white and spiraling with happiness.

CHAPTER SEVEN

asteress Meenore watched Elodie follow the high brunka into the night. What a slender reed the girl is, IT thought, and such a valiant reed! How easy to cut down a reed.

ITs smoke grayed, and something that might have been a tear filled ITs emerald eye. Never before had an unfathomably brilliant, temperamentally chilly IT so treasured a human girl.

As IT curled ITself for sleep, IT felt virtuous. I am capable of deep feeling, IT thought.

And yet I sent her into danger.

Pride in ITs goodness faded. IT thought, Life is danger, and was asleep.

CHAPTER EIGHT

igh Brunka Marya lit their way with a series of rainbows. When they reached the end of one, it faded, and she sent forth another. Snow still fell, but lazily. Beyond the rainbow glow the night was black and seemed eternal, although to the east, on the other side of the mountain, the horizon might already be smudged with gray. Elodie and High Brunka Marya crossed a wide ledge through deep snow.

"There's a stairway ahead. Hold my hand, lamb."

Their gloved hands met easily, since the two were equally tall. High Brunka Marya's grip was firm.

"Here. Up." She tugged Elodie.

Although Elodie sought footing, her boot just crashed through snow. Then she had it. She'd been feeling for something higher, but these steps had been made for short legs. They climbed together, struggling in the snow. Once, Elodie had to hold the high brunka to save her from falling. Luckily the steps were wide enough for the two to climb side by side.

A closeness comes when two do something difficult together. Elodie felt she could rely on the high brunka for steadiness, and she hoped the high brunka was beginning to trust her.

It occurred to Elodie that after the high brunka showed her the Replica's hiding place, they might not be alone together again. She tried to think of questions that a penetrating mind would ask.

Nothing came for two more steps. Then she huffed, "High Brunka, why did your worry grow when you found out I'm from Dair Mountain?"

She heard a smile in High Brunka Marya's voice. "That was before your masteress explained matters to me."

An evasion.

Two more difficult steps to another ledge. They lumbered through snow and then were out of it, under the eaves of the Oase. The high brunka let Elodie's hand go and strained to raise a heavy wooden bar, finally succeeding.

"Help me. Push!"

The big door moved by inches. Elodie doubted it would be wide enough to admit Masteress Meenore, although Count Jonty Um, whose size was mostly in height, probably could squeeze through.

They slipped in as soon as the opening let them and then had to work to close the door again. Darkness was broken only by embers glowing in three distant fireplaces, one far to the right, one far to the left, and the last far, far ahead. The space felt vast and empty and hardly warmer than the cold outside.

The high brunka took her hand again. "Come."

Elodie's feet *shushed* across the floor rushes.

"Quietly!" High Brunka Marya whispered. Her steps were noiseless.

Elodie lifted her feet but couldn't help making a small whisking sound with each footfall.

Around the fireplace in the right wall, cocooned in blankets, people, probably bees, slept on pallets, as the servants did in His Lordship's castle. One slumberer rolled over. Another flung out an arm. An old man slept sitting up on a bench next to the fire. His snore rumbled and whistled to a regular beat.

They passed the fireplace and eventually reached a smaller door, much too low and narrow for Elodie's masteress or His Lordship.

"Don't gasp," High Brunka Marya whispered.

What was there to gasp about? Elodie braced herself for a shock. The high brunka opened the door.

The air smelled metallic. Near the ceiling of a narrow

corridor that had been carved out of the mountain, wee lights twinkled.

"Lambs and calves!"

"Shh!" But the whisper sounded proud. "Oase glow-worms. Brighter than my rainbow."

"Flying worms?"

"They hang."

The worms emitted a green light. Each one was as tiny as the tip of a blade of grass, and they were as crowded together as grass in a meadow.

"They hiss," the high brunka added. "But you probably can't hear them."

She couldn't. She followed High Brunka Marya straight ahead, looking up as she walked. The glowworms continued into the distance. "Are they magic? Did Brunka Harald make them?"

"They were here before him. They're just worms."

They weren't *just* anything. "Why don't they light up the great hall?"

"They prefer smaller places." She turned right into another corridor. The worms shone here, too.

The passageway was warmer than the great hall had been, as warm as spring. Elodie let her cloak hang loose.

"Lamb . . ." The high brunka stopped. "If you want to stay here, no matter what happens with the Replica, we'll give you asylum. You don't have to continue to serve the dragon. You'll be as safe as the glowworms here."

Oh no! "Did something happen to my parents?"

"No. I believe they're fine. I didn't mean to frighten you."

"Then why would I need asylum?"

"Your parents sent you away, a twelve-year-old lamb—I mean, child."

"My parents love me!"

"You could be a bee if you like."

Elodie shrugged this off. Bees didn't mansion or deduce or induce. "High Brunka, I'm old enough to apprentice, and my family thought I could do it for free."

Her parents, with the encouragement of Albin, who knew she wouldn't live a happy life on the farm, had sent her, less than six weeks ago (although it seemed like an age) across the strait to apprentice in Two Castles town. They hadn't known what she'd learned only on her way over, that free apprenticeships had been abolished. If Masteress Meenore hadn't taken her in, she might have starved. If Count Jonty Um hadn't hired them, he'd still be just a frightening figure to her.

So much had happened, so many wonders, so much terror, but also great happiness.

"Few live the life they thought they wanted, lamb." The high brunka started walking again.

They passed six closed doors on each side.

"What rooms are these?"

"They're for guests, but they're empty now."

The Replica could be in one of them, Elodie supposed. Or it could be outside, in a tree hole or buried under earth and snow, and then how would anyone find it?

Only by luck or cleverness.

The doors ended. Other corridors branched off to the right and left, here and there, but this one continued for at least a quarter of a mile. Elodie felt the weight of the mountain press down on her. How much time had passed since she'd left her masteress? Was Zertrum's volcano already spewing?

"When I get this far, I can no longer hear a sound from the great hall, not even a shout."

"How did you hear my masteress?"

"We've been walking south, not far from the face of the mountain. I can hear the world outside. And ITs voice carries."

"How far can you hear ordinary conversation?"

"Eavesdropping is as rude as picking one's teeth!"

Elodie's smoke would have turned red if she'd had smoke. If the high brunka had been willing to be impolite, she might have heard something and prevented the theft. "If you did listen, how far could you hear?"

"About two hundred yards."

"A whisper?"

"I don't know, lamb. A hundred yards, perhaps."

"High Brunka, begging your pardon, you'll listen until the Replica is found, won't you?"

"I hadn't thought . . . It's a habit not to . . . Yes, lamb, I'll listen."

Doors began again on the left.

"We put guests in here only in summer when all the other rooms are full," the high brunka said.

"Why do you wait till then?"

"So I can sleep. My room is nearby. When these chambers are occupied, the people keep me awake, just by rolling over in their sleep. I feel like I'm in the middle of a flock of noisy pigeons."

A single door broke the right-hand wall, and it alone had a lock.

"What room is this?"

"It's a storage area."

"When the Replica was stolen before, did that high brunka keep it in the same place as you do?"

"No. Then it was on a table in the middle of the great hall. I was just a brunkle, a lamb like you. No one gave a thought to theft. It had never happened."

Another right and they reached a series of doors on either side of the corridor.

The high brunka said, "These chambers hold just relics and curiosities."

More hiding places for the Replica.

Ahead, a man and a woman sat side by side on stools. The woman kicked the man in the shins. "Get up, Johan, lazy lump." Her sharp voice seemed to strike the rock walls and bounce down the corridor.

The man stood awkwardly, without complaining. His cloak, which had been draped over his stool, slid to the ground. Grunting, he picked it up and held it bunched in his arms. Upright, he rocked back and forth on his heels, a tall, stout, ruddy-faced young man whose left cheek bulged with what was probably a toothache remedy.

Elodie expected the high brunka to tell the woman she shouldn't be kicking people, but she just said, "Why are *you* guarding, Ludda?"

Ludda-bee rose in one fluid motion for all she was middle-aged, and her cloak remained on the stool. "Deeter begged a few more minutes of sleep. Now breakfast needs starting, and where is he?" She turned to Elodie. "Everyone imposes on my good nature."

Elodie bobbed a curtsy. Do not show your penetrating mind, she thought. Do not show you think this woman has no good nature.

Wicked enough to steal the Replica?

Ludda-bee was thin with a fat face and small features—small mouth, small nose, and small eyes—crowded together in the middle of a big, round face, like a raisin roll in which all the raisins had collected in one spot. Her smile would have to be small, too, hemmed in as it was by lots of cheek. Yes, it *was* small, and the smile did nothing to banish her peevish expression. "I'm Ludda-bee."

The cook, Elodie remembered, had been there when the high brunka returned to Master Robbie without the Replica.

Ludda-bee continued. "And this shy, hulking thing is my friend Johan-bee, Johan-of-the-privy, as we bees call him."

They were friends? Elodie looked at his face—large nose, thin lips, that bulging cheek, owlish round eyes, expression blank. He doesn't consider her a friend, she concluded.

"Two nights in a row of guarding, Johan," the high brunka said. "Thank you."

His face relaxed. "You're welcome." The second word sounded like *welka*, likely because he found it hard to close his lips on the *m*.

Ludda-bee seemed to resent the compliment. "If you can call it guarding. He left me thrice to visit the garde-robe, and was, as ever, slow to return."

Elodie blushed.

"It's my stomach, Ludda."

It couldn't matter for the theft that Ludda-bee was hor-rible and that Johan-bee didn't like her. But it might matter that Johan-bee deserted his post sometimes.

"When someone tells me her name, young mistress, I always tell her mine, unless I'm a rude lout."

"Pardon!" She dropped another curtsy while hoping Ludda-bee would turn out to be the thief. "I'm Elodie."

"Come, lamb." The high brunka took her hand again. "I promised you a gift. You may have a painted rainbow."

Elodie expected to go into the room closest to the bees, which they had been guarding. But instead they turned right into an intersection after that door and entered a short corridor.

A few steps took them to a door on which words were painted in neat blue letters: *Hart Room*. Below the words, for those who hadn't learned to read, a representation of a stag in red paint. The painter was a master artist to capture the antlers, the delicate stance, the curves of back and belly, in only a few brushstrokes.

The high brunka opened the door, which had no lock, and closed it behind them. "This is my chamber. Folks see guards by the Goat Room and believe the Replica is there, but I kept it here. Anyone who plotted to steal it would be planning to take it from the wrong room."

Glowworms lit this space, too. The bedsheets and blanket were rumpled. A high brunka who didn't make her bed might like such chores as little as Elodie did. The chamber had a fireplace, which was empty, since the air was warm.

A rack, hung with spare hose and a spare shift, stood to the side of the fireplace. Elodie looked away, embarrassed to see the exalted brunka's undergarments. "Why is there a fireplace when you don't need it?"

"The early brunkas didn't know the temperature would stay warm all year. Only the great hall gets cold."

The other furnishings were a padlocked chest, a shelf above it that held a pile of small wooden arches painted in rainbow colors, a low stool, hooks on the wall, and a hanging that depicted a female brunka standing before a cottage on the Lahnt plateau. Another door, without a lock, provided a second exit.

"Where does that lead to?"

"The storage room we passed before." High Brunka Marya straightened her sheets.

Embarrassed at being caught with an untidy bed?

"The lock on the storage room door was made on the mainland. I was assured it cannot be picked. Safe as the heart in your chest, they said."

"Is the door locked on the inside, too?"

"No, lamb, only on the corridor side. If you're inside the storage room, you just lift the latch."

"Who has a key?"

The high brunka showed Elodie a large silver key among a ringful of keys fastened to her belt. "No one else has it. But if the thief was in here, picking wouldn't have been needed. My bees will search the storage area first."

Elodie felt a bubble of hope. It might be that simple. "Was the Replica in there?" She pointed at the chest.

"No, lamb. You see, my fireplace needs more daub."

Daub made of dried mud and straw cemented the stones together in a fireplace or in walls. Elodie didn't see what missing daub had to do with the Replica.

High Brunka Marya brought the stool to the fireplace and stood on it. "I don't know why I closed it up again." She began to pull out loose stones from the chimney about a foot above the mantel to reveal a hole.

Lambs and calves! If Elodie had managed to get in to this chamber and had known the Replica was here somewhere, she wouldn't have more than glanced at the chimney.

The high brunka stepped down to let Elodie see, and she climbed up, too.

There, immured in the chimney wall behind the facade of stones, was the pedestal, cloud gray marble shot through with lines of white and patches of gray and black.

"How tall is it?"

"Two and a half feet."

Elodie stuck her hand in and explored the top with her fingers: square, perhaps ten inches on a side with a three-inch groove in the middle. "Is there a ridge in the Replica that fits the slit?"

"Exactly, lamb."

"Is the magic in the pedestal?"

"I don't know, lamb. I always supposed it was in the Replica. Perhaps it's in both."

Elodie nodded, then pivoted carefully on the stool, memorizing the room for her masteress. No trapdoor in the rock floor, none in the rock ceiling. She prayed she hadn't missed anything.

High Brunka Marya's face had a listening look.

"Excuse me. Can you hear what Ludda-bee and Johan-bee are saying?" Elodie couldn't hear even a murmur. Maybe one of them had divulged something useful. "Can you hear them as clearly as you can hear me?"

The high brunka nodded. "Ludda-bee said I was kind to give you a wooden rainbow. She told Johan-bee that he was too lost in his own concerns to be as kind."

"What did he say?"

"Nothing. The tooth remedy makes speech difficult. The bees all tease him about it and other matters, although Ludda is the worst. They mean no harm. He has to learn to command respect. You know that."

Elodie nodded. Bees sometimes had to tell farmers what to do and make them do it. But the teasing still seemed cruel. Johan-bee might learn better from kindness.

The high brunka took a rainbow from the shelf. "Ludda-bee may ask to see it."

The rainbow was small enough to fit in Elodie's purse.

Her thoughts returned to the Replica. What else should she ask? She felt the usual pressure on her brain, and IT wasn't even here. "Er . . . do all brunkas know where the Replica was kept?" Probably a silly question. A brunka would never take it.

"We all know. We decided together where to put it after the first theft. Lamb, a brunka could no more harm Lahnt than a rabbit could kill a deer."

But, Elodie thought, a brunka might tell someone who could. "Are any other brunkas here now?"

"I'm the only one. My bees are all the help I need. Have you seen enough for your masteress?"

"Was anything out of place when you came in to get the Replica?"

"Nothing. The room was as it always is."

"Have you opened the chest?"

"I did. It's not there."

"I guess I've seen enough." Elodie hoped IT would know what to make of it all.

Instead of leaving, High Brunka Marya sat on the bed. A rainbow drooped from her hand. "I half convinced myself that when I came back, the Replica would be here, that I'd imagined the theft. Come, lamb." But she didn't rise. "Brunkas are kind, but we're blamers."

Elodie had to strain to hear.

"If anyone is hurt . . . if anyone . . ."—she left the

word *dies* unspoken—"I'll blame myself, and the others will blame me, too."

"You didn't steal the Replica."

"I failed to keep Lahnt safe." She stood. "And now I must confess."

CHAPTER NINE

band of gray brightened the eastern horizon as a swift settled on the slate roof of a stone cottage with two chimneys and an attached stable. Destination reached, the ogre within awakened and thought . . .

Not about Elodie or the missing Replica or even Nesspa, but about his coming nakedness. Fee fi! He had to decide quickly, because he couldn't stay himself inside a bird or beast for long. The only time he had, he'd been very ill.

He planned and concentrated so the swift would remember, and then he receded.

The bird tapped the shutters of one of the front windows of the cottage, rattling the slats and the window frame, not knowing about brunkas' sharp ears.

"Enough. I hear you." The door rumbled open as a voice

said, "Welcome. Always welcome. Enter. What's— Bird?"

A short, youngish personage—Brunka Arnulf—stood on the threshold, wearing a long undershirt with a blanket slung around his shoulders. Although he was half asleep, his expression was courteous and peaceful, and his mouth curved in a gentle smile—a brunka as brunkas normally were.

The swift flew inside and stood on the floor between an oaken table and a man sitting up on a pallet.

"Perhaps it's feeling cold," the man said.

Brunka Arnulf crouched. "Look! It's wearing Marya's medal." He held out his hand.

The bird hopped across the floor to the hand but not on it and allowed the brunka to wind the chain off his neck. Then he began to vibrate and grow.

Anticipating the worst, the man jumped up and flattened himself against the nearest wall while the brunka retreated to the doorway.

After a minute, an amber-furred monkey with a pale face and merry copper eyes smiled hugely at them both, showing an inch of pink gum. He scampered to the table and snatched up a heel of bread, which he crammed into his mouth. As soon as he swallowed, he tilted back his head and laughed a huffing, breathy laugh.

The brunka and the man smiled, although the man's smile was hesitant.

"Is it . . ." the man said.

"I think so," the brunka answered.

"Foh!" The man's smile vanished. "They eat people! Do you think it ate Marya? Is it here to eat us?"

The monkey picked up two spoons and a ladle and juggled them while continuing to laugh.

"No . . ." The brunka shook his head. "If it was going to, it would have come in its own shape."

"They're gross, monstrous."

Still laughing, the monkey darted to the brunka, pulled the blanket away from him, and dragged it outside, trailing it through snow that mounded to the monkey's waist. The brunka lifted a cloak from a peg by the door and followed at a distance. On him, the snow reached his thighs.

A dozen yards from the cottage, with his back to Brunka Arnulf, the monkey shifted, this time into Count Jonty Um. Fee fi! He hastily pulled the blanket up and tied it around his waist. The snow rose only to just above his ankles.

Bracing himself for the brunka's terror, he turned. He meant to keep his expression neutral, but a careful onlooker—Elodie or Masteress Meenore—would have seen the worry around his eyes and a smolder of resentment in the corners of his mouth. An unobservant person would have seen a glum face, not inviting, not friendly.

Brunka Arnulf didn't step forward but he didn't step back. If he felt fear, he kept the feeling in check. His voice careful, he said, "If you can be that laughing monkey, there must be some joy in you. Therefore, I'm happy to make your acquaintance. I'm Brunka Arnulf, which you may already have guessed." He bowed but kept his eyes on the ogre's face.

At the absence of fear and disgust, the face cracked into a smile that rounded His Lordship's eyebrows, lifted his cheeks, and softened his eyes. The brunka's peaceful smile widened, too, as it could hardly fail to.

"Count Jonty Um of Two Castles." His bow was a mere inclination of the shoulders. Then he shook his head, shaking the smile away. "I have terrible tidings." He explained what he knew of the theft of the Replica. "The high brunka says everyone should leave . . ." He trailed off because Brunka Arnulf had run back into the cottage.

The brunka reemerged in a minute. "Canute will begin the alarm. My other bees are helping families and flocks. If only there weren't so much snow! Will you stay to help, Master Count?"

"No. I have questions to ask you and then I must return with the answers."

"Ask." He put the high brunka's medal in his purse.

"Do you know of anyone who is angry at brunkas or anyone on Zertrum"—he didn't like asking the rest of the question because it sounded strange, but he did—"or even angry at the mountain itself?"

"You're helping Marya find the thief!"

"Yes." He didn't want to bring a dragon into the discussion. He shivered in the cold, and his stomach rumbled.

Canute-bee, casting frightened looks at His Lordship, led a horse out of the stable and mounted it. He started down the mountain, the horse making slow progress through the snow, despite Canute-bee's frantic slaps on the beast's rump.

"People are angry," Brunka Arnulf said, "then not angry, then angry again. They don't steal the Replica every time they're vexed." Thoughtfully he flicked a short rainbow out of his right hand. It hung in the air for a few seconds before fading.

His Lordship wished he'd do it again and again.

"Folks don't tell us about every argument."

"Someone did steal it," His Lordship said.

"So you say." He sighed. "Franz was angry." He explained that he had told his bees not to help a farmer named Franz after his shed burned down for the second time. "He'll be more careful in the future. He put up a new shed, which took longer without our aid, but I brought him a basket of eggs a month later. He invited me in for a meal, and we were jolly together."

"Anyone else?"

Another rainbow flashed out. "Dror."

"He's angry?"

"Maybe. Three months ago his father kicked him off his farm and made him choose to become either a bee or a soldier, and he picked bee, as I advised. He's at the Oase. Being a bee will settle him. He wouldn't steal the Replica or hurt his family. He's a loyal lad."

Meenore would want to know about this.

"Has anyone else left the mountain recently?"

"Master Uwald and Master Tuomo, his steward, rode to Zee. They'll pass the Oase going and coming back. I don't know if they'll stop. And Master Tuomo's sons are on their way to a wedding on Letster Mountain."

Count Jonty Um frowned. "Does Master Tuomo have daughters and a goodwife?"

"Just his sons. He's a widower."

"Does Master Uwald have children and a goodwife?"

"Neither. He lives with his steward and his steward's sons, and he has servants."

Meenore would be interested in this, too. "Anyone else?"

"Mistress Sirka left, but barber-surgeons never tarry long anywhere. I heard a rumor that she and Dror were betrothed, although nothing came of it."

The brunka had now answered Elodie's and Meenore's questions, but Count Jonty Um suspected Meenore would have found more to inquire about if IT had been here. A headache started, which would have felt familiar to Elodie.

"Oh!" Brunka Arnulf extended his arms, palms down, fingers spread, as if he were calming something. "Did you hear that, Master Count?"

"No."

"The volcano rumbled. It was so slight I might not have noticed if you hadn't come with your news. The Replica hasn't been found yet."

A winter hare hopped across the snow to the right of the brunka's cottage. Canute-bee would warn the humans, who would flee the mountain if they could. If they had time, they'd drive their herds and flocks along with them. His Lordship ground his teeth in misery. The wild beasts wouldn't understand the warning.

The hare stopped, nose twitching, ears straight up. His Lordship remembered being a hare and hearing thunder. His frightened hare's heart had jolted painfully before his ogre mind took over. If the tremors grew strong enough for the beasts to sense them, they'd run hither and yon, crazy with terror, but they wouldn't know to leave the mountain. If the worst happened, they'd stay and die.

CHAPTER TEN

n the corridor again, High Brunka Marya told Ludda-bee and Johan-bee to accompany her to the great hall. Once there, Ludda-bee bustled off to the kitchen. The high brunka brightened the chamber with a grand rainbow. Elodie blinked in the light, her eyelids sandy from lack of sleep.

High Brunka Marya awakened her bees and gave some of them tasks, which they began unquestioningly, although a few sent curious glances Elodie's way. The bees seemed unremarkable most in middle age, plump or thin, straight or stooped, evenly divided between men and women.

Possibly one of them had stolen Lahnt's most precious thing, but Elodie could hardly credit it. Bees helped people. They devoted their lives to helping, and most appeared to love it. They didn't need to steal because everyone contributed to the brunkas and their bees. The saying went, *One bean to the brunka, nineteen beans remain.* Lahnters gave a twentieth of everything to the brunkas and their bees. The saying continued, *They give out of goodness. We give out of gratitude.*

High Brunka Marya's rainbow dwindled as her bees lit tallow lamps and torches around the great hall, creating almost as much smoke as light. The youngest bee and the most eager, a man, hurried to the northwest corner of the great hall, where benches, stools, wooden boards, and trestles were stacked. He dragged four benches to the largest fireplace, the one opposite the entrance to the Oase, and arranged them in a line.

Elodie circled the chamber, whose immensity rivaled the great hall in Count Jonty Um's castle. She took it all in: the stone floor under a scattering of rushes; the distant stone ceiling, reinforced by oak beams; and the stone walls, interrupted at intervals by oak posts. Only the outer wall was entirely man-made, plaster over ordinary wattle and daub, broken near the ceiling by a line of eight small windows covered with the usual oiled parchment, which gleamed a gray that gave nothing away. Dawn might have begun, or it might not have. Her masteress might be here any minute or not for another hour or two.

Count Jonty Um must have reached Zertrum by now.

Was the mountain aflame? Had he learned the identity of the thief? Was he on his way back to them? Was he safe?

All four walls were lined with closed cabinets and open shelves, which held what Elodie supposed were relics of Lahnt and brunka history. The Replica could be hidden in a cabinet or even on an open shelf, concealed behind something larger. A person could spend days—a week!— combing through everything. And then there were the chambers of relics High Brunka Marya had pointed out and probably others besides. Lambs and calves! A legion of bees would be needed to search everywhere in time.

Two doors and an archway opened off the chamber: the big outside entry door in the west wall; an archway far to the left of it in the north wall; and a small door on the right side of the east wall, the door the high brunka had taken her through, which led to her distant chamber.

Johan-bee and two more bees stirred up embers in the three fireplaces and added logs until crackling and spitting spiked the quiet.

In the center of the hall, High Brunka Marya spoke softly to a knot of older bees—those, Elodie supposed, who'd been with her for at least seven years, as IT had required. She heard muffled exclamations and cries of distress. When the high brunka finished, they left the hall in pairs, except for the bee who seemed oldest. Elodie deduced the pairs were off to begin the search and perhaps to wake the guests.

On their way, a bee detoured to Johan-bee and jogged his arm so that his poker clattered on the hearthstone. Johan-bee looked up, flushing, but said nothing.

They all plague him, Elodie thought.

The oldest bee—a big man with a big head, a blood-shot nose, and a white beard trimmed straight across the bottom—shuffled to the benches that had been placed by the youngest bee. His jowls jiggled as he sat and placed his elbows on his knees, his chin in his hands, facing into the great hall, watching everyone intently.

Elodie turned to investigate the shelf nearest her, which was on the south wall. She hoped that luck might trump the arduous work of deducing, inducing, and using her common sense. Let the Replica be here!

But the shelf merely held a forest of vials made of clay and glass, none big enough to contain the Replica or to conceal it from view. The shelf below was filled with chained books, chained so they could be read but not taken away. Elodie pulled one out and proved to herself that the Replica wasn't behind it. There! She'd searched two shelves—out of hundreds—and behind one book—out of dozens.

"Son, there will be an excellent reason." The voice was soft-spoken, educated, the *t* crisply pronounced, the *r*'s solid. "High Brunka Marya wouldn't have roused us for anything insignificant."

Still holding the book, Elodie twisted to see. Only a

few yards to her left, an elderly man and a boy entered the great hall. The man held the boy's hand and advanced with small steps, as if he were walking in a slow procession.

Son? The man was old enough to be the boy's grandfather.

Was this "poor" Master Robbie? Elodie opened her book and watched the two while mansioning absorption in the volume. Both wore wooden mourning beads over their cloaks. Did the beads make them both "poor"?

Almost everything about the man was just so, and nothing suggested he'd been surprised from sleep: short gray beard and mustache, neatly clipped; small ears; thin nose onto which round spectacles were clamped. He wore a sober dark-blue cloak of brushed wool edged with a border of rabbit fur, a wealthy costume. Only his hat—wealthy also, orange with a bright-green tassel—veered, in Elodie's opinion, from *just so* to *too much*.

Could he be the thief? He seemed not to need money. If he was the thief, the just-so in him meant he would make a careful, thorough job of it.

How could a thief look so genial? He smiled as if he'd been awakened from happy dreams.

The boy's cloak, fine brushed wool also, his in moss green, lacked only a fur trim. His shoes, with the old-style round toes that were still customary in Lahnt, were so new they hardly had creases.

Below his neck, he was a just-so boy. But his unguarded face gave too much away, and its forlorn look made Elodie's breath catch.

An artist could have sketched his portrait almost entirely in straight lines: the head a triangle ending in a pointed chin, a smaller triangle for his nose, a horizontal slash for his unsmiling mouth, two angled strokes for the shadows under his cheeks, roof peaks for his eyebrows, curved lines only for his dark-blue, red-rimmed eyes and for the dot of pink that bloomed at the tip of his nose, probably caused by weeping.

Elodie bent her head over her book, not wanting to seem to pry, but the just-so man noticed her. "Look, Robbie, someone for you to play with. Isn't that lucky?"

He *was* Master Robbie!

To her surprise the boy came to her and whispered, "It's gone. Am I right?"

In a rush she induced and deduced. Master Robbie knew. He'd asked to see the Replica, and the high brunka hadn't brought it out.

Should she reveal she knew, too? Would her masteress want her to?

Probably not, but—she used her common sense—he knew everyone here, and he'd tell her more if she were honest. "Yes," she whispered back. "The high brunka told us."

Master Robbie looked around, probably seeking the rest of Elodie's *us*.

She remembered that IT wanted her to appear slow-witted, but that wouldn't do with someone her age.

"I'm Elodie of Dair, and I'm"—with a touch of grandeur—"delighted to make your acquaintance." She gave him the curtsy she had once bestowed upon Greedy Grenny, King of Lahnt.

He bowed a slight bow, the bow Count Jonty Um would make to a peasant. "I'm Robbie."

Maybe he was too sad to be polite.

"I was of Zee." Zee was the fishing village where the cog had docked. "Now I'm of Zertrum."

"Oh!" He'd lose his new home if the Replica wasn't found.

He tilted his chin toward the elderly man. "With him." He touched his mourning beads.

She said what grown-ups say: "I'm sorry for your loss."

His voice sharpened. "Whales and porpoises! I didn't *lose* anything." He was silent a moment. "I apologize. My grandmother died. She used to say I have no manners." Then he added what Elodie had heard people remark about orphans: "She was all I had in the world."

"I'm sorry," she repeated. No parents? He really was *poor* Master Robbie.

He changed the subject. "The Replica could be in a

thousand places. Have you been here before?"

She shook her head.

"There are corridors of rooms full of things like this." He gestured at the shelves in front of them.

"You think it's inside the Oase?"

"If it's outside, it could be anywhere. Something else is missing, too."

"What?"

"I'll show you."

How could he show her something that wasn't there?

CHAPTER ELEVEN

lodie?" An unmistakable round baritone. "Lady El?"

Her pet name, which she loved. "Albin? Albin!"

In an instant he rushed to her, lifted her by her waist, and spun her around, exactly as he used to after they'd mansioned a scene particularly well. When she sailed by Master Robbie, she saw his expression close.

She pitied him, but Albin came first.

He set her down.

Master Robbie left them, his shoulders hunched as he went to the just-so man, who had seated himself in the middle of the row of benches, two benches away from the elderly bee.

"Are Mother and Father here, too?"

"I'm alone. How did you get here?"

"It's too much to tell." What *could* she tell him? She could trust him with anything. Even IT would have to agree. She beckoned him to bend to hear a whisper. Certainly she could divulge this, which he'd find out soon anyway: "I came with a dragon."

Albin straightened. "No!"

Theft or no theft, she smiled her widest smile. "Yes."

He looked puzzled and pleased. "Lady El—"

There wasn't time for his questions. "Why are you here?"

"Because"—he began to narrate and mansion, as he often did—"the farmer sent his helper"—he bowed awkwardly, portraying the lowly helper of Elodie's father—"here to secure enough coin from the good brunkas for passage to Two Castles to bring his daughter back."

She'd sent a note to set their minds at rest, but it might not have reached them.

"Why didn't they ask Brunka Wilda?" She was the Dair brunka.

"Brunka Wilda said no, and so did the high brunka. They think Bettel and Han shouldn't have sent you to Two Castles."

If Elodie had had a tail, it would have twitched. The brunkas had judged without understanding.

"What is this, rousing people in the night?" The voice,

loud and angry, issued from the doorway.

Elodie turned to look.

The speaker addressed the just-so man. "Has High Brunka Marya told you, Uwald?"

Elodie tilted her head at Albin. The just-so man was Master *Uwald*? Master Uwald, the richest person on Lahnt after the earl?

Albin whispered, "The very same."

Master Uwald's vast Nockess Farm spread across the south slope of Zertrum Mountain and into the valley. With the Replica gone, he stood to lose everything.

He'd called Master Robbie *son*, but Master Uwald didn't have a son. Everyone knew that.

"Marya hasn't told us anything yet," the just-so man— Master Uwald—said, "but I'll bet it has to do with our new arrival." He gestured in Elodie's direction.

Still in the doorway, the newcomer demanded, "Who is she?"

Albin added, still whispering, "That's his steward, Master Tuomo."

Elodie curtsied. "I'm Elodie of Potluck Farm on Dair, Master."

Rudely, Master Tuomo said nothing, just swung into the great hall with a rolling gait. He reminded Elodie of the knave in a pack of cards: his cap tight against his forehead, his face any age between thirty and fifty, a thick fringe of brown beard, wary brown eyes, short neck, barrel chest, thin legs. A rich man in a brown cloak with a silver pin at the neck. He, too, wore mourning beads.

Might he be the thief? Elodie thought. If he had taken the Replica, it would have been in anger. She returned to wondering about Master Robbie. How did he and Master Uwald come to be together? Master Uwald had been jilted by his first and only sweetheart. He had no children and thus no grandchildren.

The steward sat on Master Uwald's other side from Master Robbie.

In a whisper, Albin added, "Master Uwald's true love was Master Robbie's grandmother. He's now the boy's guardian."

Everyone knew the story of young Mistress Lilli and Master Uwald and laughed over its irony. She turned down the marriage offer of a poor peddler (Goodman Uwald then) because she disapproved of wagering, and he bet on anything. Soon after, he threw the dice and won the most prosperous farm on Lahnt. He'd been rich ever since.

Was the grandson going to get the riches?

Did Master Robbie love his guardian?

Two bees entered with the barber-surgeon the high brunka had mentioned earlier, her occupation revealed by her linen cap bleached to snowy whiteness. She was a large woman, young, with ripples of light-brown hair below the cap. Her face was broad with widely spaced tawny eyes, flaring nostrils, a round chin, thick neck.

She smiled at the chamber, and the smile tightened her chin and raised her cheekbones, making her handsome. Such a smile it was, mouth half open, a blazing smile. Elodie thought, When I smile that way, I'm running full tilt or standing at the prow of the cog in a strong wind with flying fish leaping about.

The woman stood behind Master Tuomo, while the bees who'd brought her sat one full bench away from the guests.

High Brunka Marya called into the kitchen, "Ludda, come. Breakfast can wait."

Did that mean all the guests were here?

Ludda-bee, a serving spoon in one hand, entered the great hall and sat with the other bees.

"Lady El . . ." Albin bowed and held his arm out for her.

In the grand manner of mansioners promenading across a stage, they strutted to the bench, where she sat next to Master Robbie. He looked solemnly at her, seeming to take her measure.

She met his gaze. After a few seconds he blushed. They both looked away.

Albin, on her other side, leaned down to whisper, "Did you mansion at all while you were away?"

She couldn't help smiling and whispered—shame on

her—loud enough for Master Robbie to hear, too, "For the king."

"No!" Albin said.

She felt Master Robbie jerk a little and sit straighter.

"Yes, and for the princess, too."

Lodie! a nasal voice said in her mind. Remember your purpose. Observe!

The bees who'd been working here in the great hall came to the benches and sat together, along with the oldest bee, who had preceded them. At the end of the bench, Johan-bee lowered himself so awkwardly—he seemed not to look—that he fell. No one had forced him into this mishap. He'd done it by himself, but the others grinned. One said, "Hopeless." Another chimed in with "Hapless." And a third, "Useless."

Everyone faced the crackling fire. Elodie turned and saw High Brunka Marya approaching from the center of the hall.

Elodie realized she shouldn't be sitting. Masteress Meenore had instructed her to observe everyone when they heard the news, but she wouldn't be able to if she couldn't see them all. She jumped up and stood to the right of the fireplace, feeling as conspicuous as a mouse on a tablecloth. Everyone stared. Albin raised his eyebrows comically. Master Robbie continued his solemn gaze.

She scanned the people, memorizing them, beginning

with the guests on the bench closest to her: Albin at the end, dear Albin in his ancient, threadbare cloak and drawstring poverty shoes, with his worn, expressive face, the deep smile lines in his cheeks, his changeable mouth; then sad Master Robbie, interesting but unknown; just-so Master Uwald, with his arm around Master Robbie's shoulders; the steward, angry Master Tuomo, whose face had not yet relaxed.

The barber-surgeon moved to loom behind the youngest bee, the ardent young man who'd placed the benches. Why was her expression triumphant?

An empty bench separated the guests from the two full benches of bees. Elodie remembered that the most trusted of them were in pairs searching the inner chambers. She'd have no chance to observe them, although one might be the thief.

She knew the names of only two bees: clumsy Johanbee and the disagreeable cook, Ludda-bee. Two others she'd noticed before: the oldest bee, and the young bee in front of the barber-surgeon, who resembled a real bee, with a plump middle, a short neck, large dark eyes, and skinny limbs.

The high brunka came to stand between the benches and the fireplace. "Please sit, Mistress Sirka."

"Why can the girl stand and not me?" asked the barber-surgeon, who now had a name—Sirka—and a voice, hoarse, and deep for a woman.

Elodie prepared to sit on the floor, where she could still see everyone.

"She's just a lamb."

Elodie continued to stand.

Mistress Sirka shrugged and inserted herself between the eager young bee and another bee. The crowded bee benches became even more cramped.

Elodie wondered if the high brunka could hear any hearts that might be pounding and identify their owners.

Watch faces and hands, Elodie thought. Emotions declared themselves through them, as every mansioner knew.

Remember to mansion shock, yourself!

Master Tuomo, still angry, said, "I hope there's a reason—"

"I must . . ." The high brunka's mouth flattened into a line, no smile. "Oh, my dears, I regret"—she pressed her hands together. The tips of her fingers tinted rainbow colors—"to say, the Replica has been stolen."

CHAPTER TWELVE

lodie put her hands over her ears as if to block the news. Her eyes met Albin's, and his were both worried and comforting.

Master Robbie watched her, too. His face was puzzled. He was probably wondering why she was shamming surprise.

Master Tuomo rose. The skin around his lips had paled. "Uwald, we can be on the road within the hour."

No one can go! Elodie thought.

"Please sit," High Brunka Marya said.

"My sons!" He remained standing. "I won't reach them in time as it is. Uwald, we must—"

"Sit." The high brunka's soft voice held a note of command.

The steward sat slowly.

His sons are on Zertrum? Elodie thought. He can't be the thief then.

Watch the bees, she told herself. IT suspects them the most. Keeping her eyes wide, her mouth sad, she turned their way.

The young bee jumped up, sat down, pumped his knees in agitation, his face tragic. Next to him, the barber-surgeon, Mistress Sirka, put a consoling arm around his shoulders. Her face looked untroubled, happy even. He seemed unaware of her.

A female bee put her fist in her mouth. Her eyes filled with tears.

The ancient bee half closed his eyes, although his face was alert.

Ludda-bee snapped, "If Johan could keep to his post, this wouldn't have happened."

First to blame. Was she directing attention away from herself? Or did she have a reason for the accusation, beyond the fact that he visited the privy while guarding? Surely everyone did that during a long watch.

The other bees seemed distressed in varying degrees, but neither their expressions nor their hands proclaimed anything definite—or anything Elodie could discern. Perhaps her masteress would already have named the thief if IT were here.

She turned from the bees back to the guests.

The genial expression had drained from Master Uwald's face. His eyes were squeezed shut. "Oh. Oh." But then they popped open. With a visible effort he brought his smile back. He stroked the top of Master Robbie's head and murmured something to him, which Elodie deduced must be an assurance that all would turn out well.

Master Robbie nodded while looking straight ahead. If he had any affection for his guardian, he was keeping the feeling to himself. His sad face was no sadder than it had been, but, of course, he'd already known.

"I'll stand with you." Albin put an arm around Elodie's shoulders and whispered, "How strange that you arrived for this. Is there"—he paused dramatically—"more to be revealed?"

Much more. She whispered back, "All will be told in the final act."

"No one has left the Oase," High Brunka Marya continued, "so one of you has the Replica or has hidden it. If you expect to profit from it, expect otherwise. We'll catch you as a hawk catches a squirrel. Even if you leave Lahnt, we'll find you and deliver you to the earl."

The earl, who administered the king's justice on Lahnt, wasn't known for his mercy.

"But if the Replica is returned before anyone on

Zertrum is hurt, then I won't seek you out. You'll have the satisfaction of having stolen it and no one—"

Master Tuomo stepped backward over the bench. "Uwald! We must leave. High Brunka, you know we must."

Master Uwald stood, too. "Yes, yes. Robbie—"

"Sit, both of you. I've sent someone to warn Brunka Arnulf. He'll raise the alarm."

Had Count Jonty Um issued the warning by now? Was he on his way back? Elodie looked up at the distant windows to see if they'd lightened with dawn, and choked back a gasp. They had brightened, except one, which was emerald green. Pressed against the window, ITs eye.

Master Uwald sat.

Master Tuomo remained standing. "No one can travel fast enough to reach Zertrum in time."

"This messenger will." The high brunka didn't explain.

Elodie hoped mention of a mysterious messenger would discomfit the thief, and perhaps it had, but everyone appeared equally dazed.

"Sit, Master Tuomo. No one may leave. The rooms of all the guests are being searched right now. Yours, too, Mistress Sirka."

The barber-surgeon stiffened. "Hair and teeth! They can't! Not without me looking on!"

"Mistress Sirka, dear lioness, they're interested in nothing but the Replica."

What in her belongings did Mistress Sirka want to keep secret? Elodie wished she could be there for the search—and here, too.

"If anything is harmed, I'll lop off someone's ear."

High Brunka Marya seemed unconcerned.

"Who will search the bees' belongings?" Master Tuomo asked. "You can't leave anyone out."

Master Uwald agreed. "The game should be fair."

Was everything with him a game to bet on, even the destruction of his farm?

"Bees have nothing of their own," High Brunka Marya said.

"They have their pallets," Master Robbie said.

Brave, to disagree with the high brunka! Elodie thought.

He went on. "Don't they sleep on the same one every night? The Replica could be stowed in a mattress. It would fit."

IT would admire that observation, Elodie thought.

Master Uwald did. "Well done, Robbie!"

Master Robbie's hand found his mourning beads. Elodie wondered if praise reminded him of his grandmother.

Mistress Sirka chimed in. "They have spare shifts, hose,

undershirts, and boots for the snow. The Replica would fit in a boot."

"The bees are searching in pairs. Mistress Sirka, you may go through the bees' things with Master Tuomo. Master Uwald, dear, if you would be so kind as to search with Goodman Albin." She didn't mention Elodie or Master Robbie.

Albin bowed at Master Uwald. "At your service."

"You may begin after we've finished talking," the high brunka said.

Albin said, "Suppose the Replica is found by a person who isn't the thief. Should he bring it to you? He won't know where it used to be kept."

Elodie felt a shiver of fear. Why did Albin think of this? The thief would definitely pretend not to know.

"Bring it to me."

"Will you believe the finder, High Brunka?" Mistress Sirka asked.

"If no one has been hurt on Zertrum, I won't care."

"Will there be a reward?"

"Robbie!" Master Uwald said.

"Your farm may be destroyed. You may be poor," he said, sounding untroubled. "I may be poor again. There should be a reward."

Elodie thought he was right. "Everything possible should be done to recover the Replica."

But High Brunka Marya tightened her lips. "Saving a mountain will be the reward."

"I'll give a reward." Master Tuomo stood again and surveyed the guests and bees. "A hundred silver coins, all my money in the world."

A fortune. The Replica was worth more, but if the thief preferred not to kill people and beasts, he or she might take the reward instead.

Elodie's head swam. Was Master Tuomo trying to save his sons—or turning suspicion away from himself?

He added, "If anybody finds the Replica, bring it to High Brunka Marya, and I'll promise you the reward. Uwald will vouch that my word is good. If you know something, tell me, and if it leads to the Replica, I'll pay you."

Master Uwald said, "I'll pay the reward, Tuomo. I can afford it better than you."

High Brunka Marya looked up at the cciling as if she might see Brunka Harald's ghost floating there. "Thank you both, but the hundred silvers will come from brunkas, and information will be delivered to me."

"What are we to do after we search the bees' things? I won't sit still."

"Dear Master Tuomo, you may look where you like, so long as you do so in the pairs I named, and so long as you remain in this chamber. And a . . . er . . . *personage* will arrive soon to speak with each of you, a personage adept at finding lost objects."

"Who?" Master Tuomo demanded.

White smoke wreathed the entry door.

"The one who brought me to the Oase." Elodie let pride infuse her voice, although she shouldn't have, since she hoped to appear dull witted. "Lahnt is lucky. Masteress Meenore is here."

CHAPTER THIRTEEN

ith the sympathy of a brunka, Brunka Arnulf brought out a meal for Count Jonty Um. The ogre devoured half a wheel of cheese, two loaves of bread, and a bunch of late carrots, and drank two pitchers of cider, dining as quickly as he could while preserving his noble manners. When he finished, although he longed to sleep in a warm place, he shape-shifted into a swift again and flew.

Dawn had just begun.

If His Lordship hadn't been tired, if his mind hadn't been sluggish with food, if he had been a bird more often, he would have remembered that dawn was the hunting hour and would have waited before shape-shifting.

As the swift rounded the eastern slope of Zertrum, an arrow pierced his shoulder, and he fell.

CHAPTER FOURTEEN

"There once was a dragon called Roarer
who filled the people with horror.
Their fear pleased IT mightily,
IT flamed at them frightfully
and caused a boisterous furor."

Enh enh enh.

No one else laughed. Elodie smiled, while wishing her masteress would stop amusing ITself.

ITs head, shoulders, and forelegs (ITs arms, as Elodie thought of them) inched gingerly into the Oase. "I will not force the matter," IT said when ITs sides filled the opening.

Everyone but Elodie, Albin, and High Brunka Marya rushed to the opposite wall.

Master Robbie took a few hesitant steps forward, managing to look at once afraid, curious, and hopeful.

High Brunka Marya said, "IT's going to help us find the Replica. IT's as clever as a ratcatcher."

"I am assuredly cleverer than that. Thief, you may confess now and save me the trouble of smoking you out, so to speak." *Enh enh enh.*

Elodie scanned the bees and guests. If she had stolen the Replica and had never encountered a dragon before, her knees would have buckled. But everyone remained upright, looking equally terrified.

IT grinned, showing ITs teeth, which were pointy as spikes.

The high brunka said, "IT wishes to speak with some of my bees first. Um . . . Ursa, take the first turn. I expect you—bees and guests—to be frank with IT, as open as children."

Elodie thought the high brunka didn't know many children.

"Share everything, even your suspicions, no matter how absurd you think they are."

Ursa-bee, as it turned out, was the bee Elodie had noticed weeping with her fist in her mouth when the high brunka had announced the theft. She was a woman of middle height, neither thin nor fat, probably in her mid-twenties, with a high forehead, thin nose, and receding chin. Her pale green eyes contrasted with her dark skin. She crept forward, her hands clasped prayerfully.

"Everyone else, in the pairs I named, can help with the search. Give the masteress and Ursa a wide berth for their private conversation. I'll be watching and listening." She drew a stool from the pallet corner into the center of the great hall.

While Ursa approached IT with slow steps, Master Robbie grabbed Elodie's hand. "I'll show you what else is missing, and what's still there."

His hand was gloved, as hers were. How bold of him to take her hand!

"Wait!" She pulled free and tried to catch ITs eye to see if she should go or stay and listen to the interviews, but IT stared fixedly at Ursa-bee. "All right. Show me."

And, she thought, tell me what you know about everyone.

CHAPTER FIFTEEN

Ts smoke rose in white spirals. People to frighten, a puzzle to untangle—bliss. Begin with an accusation: "You are from Zertrum, are you not?"

Ursa-bee shook her head so hard her cap trembled.

"From where then?"

She swallowed several times. "From Dew."

"This Dew is hard upon Zertrum? In the shadow of the volcano?"

"N–no! It's the north harbor village, Sir—M–Mistress—Masteress."

"Yes, *Masteress.* That is the correct appellation. You despise being a bee?"

"No!" Vehemence seemed to give her courage. "Anywhere else I'd be just a maid of all work. Here I dust, mop, help with the laundering, sweep up the old rushes, put down the new, as a maid would, but I also take my turn guarding the Replica."

"You regard your fellow bees highly?"

She smiled, revealing small and uneven teeth. "Certainly! They're bees. They want to help Lahnt. Some come from rich families and could have been anything. Dror was offered the choice of soldier or bee, and he chose bee."

Which might merely mean, IT thought, he preferred not to die. "In the while since Master Robbie arrived, have you guarded the Replica?"

"Three times, Masteress."

Now to the heart of it. "Did anything out of the ordinary occur?"

She turned to see where the high brunka was, still on her stool, too far away for a human to hear but doubtless an easy listening distance for a brunka. The bee's fear had come back. "We didn't t-tell Marya because all seemed well."

"Tell her what?"

"Yesterday morning, after six, soon after Marya left her bed, late into our watch, Johan went to the garderobe, as he often does before the end of a watch. He's always very slow there. Everyone teases him, but I rarely do, because he suffers so. When he'd been gone a minute or two, I heard weeping from the next corridor, the most piteous weeping. I tried not to move but I had to look. Sir . . ."

IT held up a claw.

"Oh. Masteress, I had to see who was crying. The sound was so sad."

The high brunka's posture stiffened. She was certainly hearing this confession that the Replica had been left unguarded.

Ursa-bee continued. "I hurried. Then I didn't find any-one, but the weeping went on and on."

Mmm.

"I thought the sound came from one of the rooms. It wormed its way into my head until I couldn't tell if it was in me or out of me, and I started crying, too. I opened door after door and found no one. Finally it died away."

"And you returned to your post?"

"I waited a few minutes, hoping to find whoever it was."

"Did you hear footsteps?"

"I couldn't hear anything over the crying. When it stopped I heard none."

"Mmm."

"Johan and I got back at the same time."

"Were you both coming from the same direction? Had he heard the weeping, too?"

"He said he hadn't. I came from the east, he from the west."

IT scratched ITs earhole. "You said all was well?"

"The Replica was still in its place. We made sure of that. If only it hadn't been!" She twisted the edge of her cloak. "We would have discovered the theft immediately."

"Describe where it was kept, if you please."

Ursa-bee looked nervously at the high brunka, who nodded. "It's in—it *was* in Marya's chamber." She went on to explain.

Very likely, IT thought, that the thief had been in the chamber, under the bed, behind a screen, somewhere! He or she had waited for the two foolish bees to leave and then made off with the prize. How remained to be discovered.

"Have you told anyone?"

"Only you." She shrugged. "And now Marya."

"Has Johan-bee?"

"I don't know, but he doesn't say much, and he has a toothache. The barber-surgeon changes the medicine every so often. He may have told her."

"Have you ever held the Replica in your hand?"

"A few times, Masteress."

"If you were the thief, could you conceal it on your person?"

"I'm not!"

IT stared at her with ITs flat, emerald gaze. "Could Johan-bee conceal it on his person?"

"If he held it under his cloak. But we don't wear our cloaks when we guard. The corridor is too warm."

Mmm. "After your watch, what did you do?"

"Ludda gave us pottage in the kitchen. Everyone else had already eaten. Then she asked us to help her dig up the last beets." Ursa-bee giggled. "Johan went to the garde-robe again before going out. We didn't wait for him, but he joined us eventually. We harvested the beets and brought them in in two baskets. Afterward, I slept until afternoon."

IT exhaled a long stream of white smoke. Progress had been made. "Send me another bee. Send me this Johan-bee."

CHAPTER SIXTEEN

 hunter picked up the wounded bird, who began to vibrate and grow. Frightened, the man let go and jumped away.

After a minute a naked ogre with a bloody shoulder faced the hunter. His Lordship blushed from his toes to his forehead. His shoulder hurt, but he wouldn't die of a single arrow. He wouldn't die of the man's fear, either. "I'm Count Jonty Um."

The man gaped.

"Of Two Castles. Your horse isn't afraid of me." He reached out and took the man's bow. "I've come to warn people. The Rep—"

The hunter's knees buckled, and he fainted.

"May I borrow your cloak?" His Lordship rolled the man over gently. Poor-quality wool, but it would have to do. "I'll pay for the garment." He tied the cloak around his waist. Then he cleaned his puncture wound with a handful of snow. The cold stung. His shoulder ached.

What to do? The arrow had dropped the swift. If he shifted back, he wouldn't be able to fly.

Elodie and Meenore needed to know that a man called Dror had been as good as forced to become a bee, and that someone named Tuomo and his sons, and someone named Uwald, had left the mountain.

If he walked, the snow wouldn't slow him greatly. The cold posed a greater danger. At best, he'd be several days getting back to the Oase. Fee fi! He was failing his friends.

He started down the mountain and stumbled out of weariness and pain. Before anything, he had to rest. He scanned the way below, but a forest blocked his view. Boulders dotted the slope above, as if a giant (much bigger than himself) had smashed a cliff and scattered the debris.

A mink stood in the shadow of a boulder, sniffing the air. This animal at least he could save. He crouched and held out his hand.

A minute later, the mink was in it. He placed the creature on his shoulder and thought, I have room for more.

Sleep first.

Between himself and the forest, three boulders leaned against one another, forming a three-sided recess that would protect him from the wind. He curled up inside, with the mink tucked between his neck and his shoulder, each giving a little warmth to the other.

He hoped that Elodie and Meenore were discovering on their own what he'd learned and that both were safe. But his last thought, before diving into a dream of snow and ice, was for Nesspa.

CHAPTER SEVENTEEN

aster Robbie led Elodie down the same corridor she'd walked earlier with the high brunka. As the air warmed, both removed their cloaks and gloves.

"A dragon brought you here?" Master Robbie asked. "On ITs back?"

"In an oxcart. The oxen pulled IT and me."

"Oh." He sounded disappointed.

A dragon wasn't enough? She had to be flying, too? "With an ogre." Why did she want to astonish him?

To distract him from his sadness?

To boast?

She shouldn't have mentioned His Lordship.

"Whales and porpoises!"

She smiled. "Yes."

"Where is he?"

Too late not to say. "He shape-shifted into a bird. He's the one who's warning the brunka on Zertrum. Then he's coming back here." Soon, she hoped. "His dog is in the stable."

"Are you afraid of him?"

"The dog or the ogre?"

He grinned. "Not the *dog*."

She grinned, too. "His Lordship is kinder than anyone I know. He hates when people fear him."

"His *Lordship*?" Master Robbie radiated disbelief.

"Count Jonty Um. You'll see. He'll tell us how things stand on Zertrum."

At the corridor that led to the high brunka's chamber, they turned left instead of right.

"Er . . . who do you think took the Replica? You know them all."

"No, I don't. I'm not sure I've even seen every single bee."

"Then among the ones you know, bees and guests."

He stopped walking and frowned at her. "You want me to accuse someone?"

She felt a rush of shame. "No. . . ." Defiance came next. "Yes. . . . Someone did it." Should she tell him she was ITs assistant?

"Who do *you* think?"

"I just got here!"

"Arriving right after the high brunka found out it was missing."

Did he suspect her?

She said, "I suspect everyone."

"Me?"

She smiled mysteriously. "Everyone." But she didn't, or didn't much. After all, he caused the theft to be discovered.

"Here we are."

The words *Squirrel Room* as well as a plump squirrel had been painted on the door, which Master Robbie pushed open. They entered a low chamber, roughly circular, lit by glowworms and cozily warm, as the corridor had been. Elodie yawned, because of the warmth and the night without sleep.

Except for four small tables, which stood apart and leaned crookedly on the uneven stone floor, the Squirrel Room was unfurnished. Atop each of three tables rested a wooden box—pale wood with flecks of paint clinging to the grain, as if they had been painted an eternity ago. The fourth table held nothing.

"Is that what's missing? A box?"

He nodded.

"Do you know what was in it?"

"First look in the ones that are here."

She went to the nearest table.

"No. That one first." He pointed.

She went to that table. "Open it?"

He nodded.

It was the width and length of her forearm, adequate to hold the Replica. Could it be in here, and he'd known all along? His face was happy, as if something lovely were about to happen.

What would he think lovely?

Uneasily, she imagined opening the box and finding a dreadful surprise, like a scorpion. The lid was hinged and fastened with a tiny hook. She nudged the hook aside. Nothing happened. She lifted the lid. Inside lay a shriveled-up daffodil.

"A flower coffin?"

"Touch it."

"Lambs and calves!"

The flower began repairing itself. Its stem and leaves lightened to a fresh spring green; its petals softened and turned the lemon yellow of the newly opened flower. When the transformation was complete, she heard laughter. The flower began to laugh—the sound couldn't have come from anywhere else.

First there were low burbles, as if something were very funny but the flower was trying not to give way to it. Then the battle was lost, and the laughter came pouring out.

Elodie grinned. How amusing, a laughing daffodil. How strange at this terrible time.

Master Robbie was chuckling. His expression softened when he laughed. Before the laughter entirely took her over, Elodie thought she might be seeing him as he'd looked before Goodwife Lilli died.

Great whoops of laughter burst from them. Master Robbie covered his mouth with his hands. Seeing him laugh that way, as if he could cram the mirth back in, made her laugh harder.

Their shoulders shook. Nothing was funny. A mountain was going to explode. People might die. Even now, His Lordship might be in danger.

But a laughing flower was funny. The muscles in Elodie's sides hurt.

Finally, the daffodil subsided, exactly the way a person does. It was quiet until a fresh giggle burst out, and then it stopped, and then started again. The bursts became shorter and the intervals longer until it was completely silent. A few moments later it began to shrivel again. Another minute, and it was as they'd found it.

Elodie's and Master Robbie's laughter diminished, too, then ceased.

"If it's touched again, it will start again."

She wondered if she could make people laugh, too. Although the flower was magical, this seemed a mansioner's sort of skill. She pushed a bubble of laughter out. Master Robbie smiled. She continued with another bubble.

He chuckled. "Whales and porpoises! You're as good as the flower."

She continued, and soon they were both roaring with laughter again. After a minute or two, Elodie, with difficulty, made her laughter die down. Gradually they both stopped.

Soberly, meeting her eyes, Master Robbie said, "Grandmother said I'd find surprising comforts."

Me? Elodie blushed and wished she could mansion a blush away.

He was blushing, too. "Open another box."

"Which?"

He pointed.

"Who showed them to you?"

"The high brunka took me and Master Uwald around the Oase the day after we came. I liked this room best."

The next box was as long as the first and a few inches wider. "Oh!" Inside lay the skeleton of some small creature. Would it come to life, too, if she touched it?

But what did this have to do with the Replica and the danger on Zertrum?

She remembered her masteress telling her not to hurry. *If you rush, you will bungle,* IT had said.

She would be patient. She touched the skeleton as lightly as she could.

At once it quivered, shivered, trembled, fluttered, became a dazzle of motion that gained bulk, feathers, a beak, claws, and shiny eyes, and finally settled down. A nightingale.

It chirped, then broke into full-throated nightingale song. After a few minutes it stopped and sagged. She touched it again to keep it alive.

When it stopped for the second time and she reached out, Master Robbie caught her hand. "I doubt it's really alive."

His fingers were warm. She swallowed hard and nodded, trying to ignore the hand. "Do you think Brunka Harald put a spell on it and the flower?"

"High Brunka Marya didn't know. She said he brought them with him to Lahnt."

He let her hand go. "Try that one."

This box was the biggest of all, square, probably a foot by a foot. A flower, a bird. What could this one be the remains of?

A wooden puppet had been folded in, facedown, ragged hat tilted up, a threadbare tunic clinging to its narrow back.

Master Robbie touched the puppet, and it popped up so that it seemed to be sitting in the box. Its long chin and even longer nose almost met. As they watched, its face became painted a cream color with scarlet spots on its cheeks and scarlet lips. Its eyes filled in with black, evenly surrounded by ivory white, like an owl's eyes.

"It looks cheerful," Elodie said.

"Or spiteful."

The jaws moved. The lips were rigid, so its smile didn't change. "I am cheerful."

Elodie gasped. It sounded uncomfortably human, speaking with a deep, velvety voice that had a happy lilt, the pitch rising on *ful* in *cheerful*. "Ask me a question."

She said, "Who took the Replica?"

Master Robbie said, "Where is it?"

It raised and lowered knobby shoulders. "The two questions I may not answer."

"What's my name, Sir Puppet?" asked Elodie.

"You go by more than one."

"Say one of them."

Its jaw clacked wordlessly. Then, finally: "Lady El."

"Lambs and calves!"

"Who made you?" Master Robbie asked.

"A wizard. I have his voice."

Elodie and Master Robbie both asked, "Do you have his powers?"

Elodie stopped breathing, waiting for the answer. Maybe the puppet could change the spell on Zertrum.

"I have knowledge but no power."

Elodie cried, "You know who took the Replica and where it is but you can't say?"

It sagged. Its paint began to peel. Quick as quick, she touched it.

It started over. "Ask me a question."

She said, "Is it true that you know who took the Replica and where it is but you can't say?"

"Yes. I know and cannot say." The voice still rose gaily at the end.

Useless thing! Elodie wanted to punch the puppet back into the box and slam the cover shut.

Master Robbie, cooler than she, said, "Can you give us a hint?"

The head nodded bumpily. "A single hint. Lady . . ." It drooped.

They both touched it.

"Ask me a question."

"Can you give us a hint?" Master Robbie said.

"About what?"

Say something useful, Elodie prayed. "About where the Replica is or who took it?"

"Expectation misleads."

Master Robbie sounded disgusted. "What use is that?"

"Whose expectation?" asked Elodie.

"Yours. And your masteress's." In ITs nasal voice, the puppet added, "Think, Lodie!"

CHAPTER EIGHTEEN

lodie couldn't imagine what the hint meant, and being commanded in ITs voice didn't help. They let the puppet return to its worn-out state.

She looked at the empty table. "Did High Brunka Marya say what was in the missing box?"

"The handkerchief that weeps, like the flower that laughs."

"How long has it been gone?"

He shook his head. "High Brunka Marya was surprised it wasn't there, but she didn't say the last time she'd seen it."

"We can ask her. We should go back." Maybe Masteress Meenore had found the Replica. Perhaps His Lordship had returned.

He pulled open the door and held it for her.

She walked slowly. "Can I trust you with a secret? You can't tell anyone."

"What secret?"

"Promise?"

He nodded.

"I'm helping IT find the Replica." Why did this feel like boasting when it was true?

Master Robbie's voice was gentle. "We're all helping IT, aren't we?"

He doesn't believe me, she thought. "Yes, of course." She resisted the impulse to tell him she was ITs paid assistant, but she couldn't help adding, "In Two Castles I helped IT find the ogre when he'd turned himself into a mouse and we thought a cat had eaten him."

"Where was he?"

"In the king's menagerie. He'd shifted into a monkey." There was much more to the story than that.

"You've seen him shape-shift?"

She described it. "It looks painful. Um . . ." She stopped walking.

He stopped, too.

"If we're all trying to find the Replica"—she couldn't think of a way to say it except straight out—"would you tell me about the people here and your opinion of them? You don't need to accuse anyone."

"Grandmother says"—his chest expanded in a deep

breath—"*used to say . . .*" He smiled at the memory. "She said that gossip is the pepper of conversation, and we don't have to be rich to enjoy it."

Only the wealthy could afford pepper for their food.

"My mother says that, too." Elodie took a chance and pried. "Goodwife Lilli wasn't wealthy?"

"Poor as an empty fishhook. She also said she'd forgo gossip pepper and take gold."

"Your grandmother must have been merry company."

"She disliked gloom." He looked down at his tunic and cloak. "Master Uwald got all this for me in Zee." He changed the subject. "Ask me your questions."

"What do you make of . . ." Which one should she start with? She wanted to know about Master Uwald, but that was mere curiosity, since he was too rich to need the Replica. "Ludda-bee?"

"The cook. She can cut steel with her tongue, but she prepares the best pottage I've ever tasted."

"Do you think she took the Replica?"

"Only if she could make someone else seem foolish, particularly Johan-bee."

"What about him? I think High Brunka Marya should stop the teasing."

"They're unkind, but he can't take a step without a misstep. Grandmother would call him 'a temptation to cruelty.'"

"Could he have taken it?"

"He'd bungle it, drop it, and everyone would hear, or he'd hide it where it would be easily found."

"Ursa-bee?"

He started walking again without answering. After a few steps he said, "If somebody can be too sweet, she's the one. She pats my shoulder every time she comes near me. I wish she'd hover over someone else. She wouldn't take the Replica, though. She wouldn't let other people suffer."

Unless she was mansioning her pity.

A bell clanged, making the glowworms flicker.

"Breakfast," Master Robbie said, walking faster.

Elodie's appetite woke up, roared, and sped her feet. In a minute they'd be back in the great hall, and maybe His Lordship would be there.

But she and Master Robbie wouldn't be able to speak openly. "What about the youngest bee, the one who was more distressed than anyone but Master Tuomo? The barber-surgeon put her arm around his shoulders."

"Dror-bee? He comes from Zertrum."

Three from Zertrum. Was that odd?

Master Robbie added, "He's excitable. When he stands, he's on his toes; when he sits at the table, he tilts into it. He talks to guests more than most bees do."

"You notice as much as a mansioner."

He looked pleased. "Mistress Sirka is sweet on him."

"Sweet on a bee?" Bees couldn't marry unless they stopped being bees.

"He's new. Maybe she knew him before."

Barber-surgeons traveled to do their work. They cut hair, pulled teeth, set bones, dosed people with herbs, and stitched up cuts.

Master Robbie continued. "I don't know how long she's been here. I imagine she gave Johan-bee his toothache remedy. Yesterday she trimmed Master Tuomo's beard and Deeter-bee's beard and toenails."

"Deeter-bee?" She remembered the bee with the beard trimmed straight across the bottom. "Is he the oldest bee?"

Master Robbie nodded. "The historian of Lahnt."

Elodie wondered if the details of the first theft might help them.

The door to the great hall was only a few yards away. "Is Dror-bee sweet on Mistress Sirka?"

"I see her watching him, but he doesn't watch her."

From inside the great hall a nasal voice sang another ditty.

There was no time now, but Elodie wished she'd had the time to ask about Master Tuomo and the courage to ask about Master Uwald. She thought, Are you safe with him, Master Robbie?

They entered.

CHAPTER NINETEEN

His Lordship surfaced from deep sleep and opened his eyes.

Fee fi! A net had been draped over the boulders. Six men stood outside, arrows nocked and aimed at him. Fo fum! A dead mink lay over the shoulder of one of them.

The hunter who'd shot the swift cried, "Ready!"

Before they could shoot, His Lordship bellowed, "Brunka Arnulf!"

The mountains carried the echo: *Brunka Arnulf.*

No one released an arrow. No one lowered his bow.

His Lordship spoke as softly as he could, explaining why he'd come to Zertrum and why Brunka Arnulf had been convinced he meant no harm. No one answered, as if he were speaking a foreign tongue, as if he were a talking bear, but a man was dispatched on horseback to find the brunka or Canute-bee.

More delay. The morning was half over.

The weak November sun failed to penetrate His Lordship's shelter, and the hunter had reclaimed his cloak.

"I need a fire or I'll be useless," Count Jonty Um said. Nesspa, he thought, I miss you. Meenore, Elodie, if the mountain spews, you'll never know what happened to me or why I didn't return.

CHAPTER TWENTY

is Lordship wasn't in the great hall. Disappointment made Elodie more tired than before.

IT was eating—and singing again.

"There once was a dragon called Aidan
who ceased dining on maiden,
preferring cabbage and beets,
ITs new delectable treats,
Deep-fried so they tasted like bacon.

"Ah, Mistress Elodie and the young squire have returned to breakfast with us."

Calling her *Mistress Elodie* hid their connection—clever, but now, she realized, Master Robbie wouldn't believe she was assisting IT in any extraordinary way.

A long board had been set on trestles near the front door so Masteress Meenore could partake. IT filled the head of the table, facing into the chamber, and High Brunka Marya perched on a tall stool at the foot. Bees and guests sat on benches on either side, all apparently having lost their fear of IT.

Albin's face brightened when he saw Elodie. "The heroine returns." He slid to make room for her in the middle of a bench, and she sat close enough to him that Master Robbie could squeeze in, too.

Master Uwald's expression also lightened. "You've made a friend, Robbie?"

Master Robbie shrugged, his eyes on IT, his expression rapt.

Albin filled a bowl for Elodie, and Master Uwald, across the table, heaped one for Master Robbie.

"We may as well eat." Master Tuomo cut himself a chunk of bread. "My sons will soon die, but we may as well eat. The land we've devoted our lives to will vanish, but we may as well eat." He bit into the bread. "Everything tastes like sawdust."

"Like sawdust?" Ludda-bee said. "What a thing to say!"

Elodie ate hungrily, passing food to diners nearby and accepting tidbits in return, as was the custom. The meal was a feast: fresh beets in cream sauce, pickled cabbage, pottage with lentils, goat cheese, and bread.

As a defense against the charge of sawdust, Ludda-bee recounted every step in her cooking: repeatedly brining the cabbage, skimming the cream for the beets, peeling each lentil.

When she drew breath, Master Robbie said, with his eyes still on IT (Elodie wondered how his spoon found his mouth), "The handkerchief that weeps still has not been returned."

"Mmm. A handkerchief that weeps?" ITs eyes touched Ursa-bee and lingered on Master Robbie. "How useless for wiping tears." IT ate the same meal everyone else shared, as well as a branch of a pine tree, which IT must have brought in. Habitually, IT dined on human food as well as wood, although IT detested oak. When IT felt light, IT downed pebbles. On occasion, knives became irresistible, though they made IT queasy.

Elodie watched everyone, remembering what Master Robbie had told her. The barber, Mistress Sirka, sat next to Dror-bee and passed him the best in her bowl. Without a doubt, she doted on him.

He seemed lost in misery, eyes down, tears streaming, hardly eating, merely pushing his spoon through his pottage. Too much sadness? Elodie wondered.

Unlike Dror-bee, Ursa-bee (the bee Master Robbie called *too sweet*) seemed to have recovered her composure. "Ludda, these are the best beets I've ever tasted."

Deeter-bee, the historian, ate at a slow, steady pace. Crumbs and flecks of food dropped into his beard and onto his cloak. "Fascinating times."

"Deeter, dear!"

"I didn't wish it to happen, Marya. But since it has, I'm glad to be a witness."

"A pox on you then." Master Tuomo stood. "I've eaten my fill, and I can't be idle. Mistress Sirka, will you search with me again?"

"I'm still eating." She spooned cabbage into Dror-bee's bowl.

Master Tuomo sat again and put his head in his hands.

IT turned to the high brunka. "The girl slept not at all last night. Goodman Albin, you are in charge of her now, but I suggest she rest an hour or two."

At this, Elodie couldn't hold back a yawn.

IT continued. "Afterward, I request her attendance in the stable. There is a dog for whom we are jointly responsible who needs exercise I cannot provide. Do you acquiesce?"

Albin nodded. "As you wish." If he realized that more lay behind the stable visit than a dog, he didn't show it. "Lady El, may your slumber be sweet."

The high brunka told Ursa-bee to take Elodie to a room. "Give the lamb the Donkey."

IT insisted that another bee go along. "Pairs, High

Brunka Marya, will spare us wondering what Ursa-bee did alone on her return."

Ursa-bee protested. "I'd come right back!"

"Apologies." The high brunka assigned Johan-bee to accompany them.

Ludda-bee's voice followed them out. "Don't fall over your feet, Johan."

Elodie followed the bees through the archway on the north wall, which led into the kitchen. She formed a quick notion of the chamber: two fireplaces, sundry shelves and cabinets (possible hiding places for the Replica), pots and pans hanging on hooks from the ceiling beams, a long oak worktable upon which rested a brass handbell, a loaf of bread, a bowl of unpeeled beets, and a pitcher—a wealthy kitchen, almost as fine as His Lordship's.

Johan-bee's hip bumped the table and made the wooden legs stutter on the stone floor.

"Johan, Johan," Ursa-bee said in a sugary voice that annoyed Elodie and must have infuriated him.

They exited through a door on the east wall. Outside, they followed a short corridor straight ahead and then turned left, the opposite direction from the high brunka's chamber, into a region of the Oase Elodie hadn't yet penetrated. As they walked, she hatched a plan to search the other guests' rooms. She probably wouldn't find the Replica, since bees had already looked, but doubtless she'd find clues. IT would be pleased.

They progressed down a corridor lit by glowworms: unbroken wall on the left, a series of closed doors on the right.

"What are these rooms for?"

Ursa-bee answered. "They hold relics and books."

"Are all the walls in the Oase made of stone?"

Ursa-bee stopped to think. Johan-bee continued for a few steps, then waited.

"All," Ursa-bee said, "except the one in the great hall that faces out of the mountain."

"The floors and ceilings are carved out of rock, too," Johan-bee added.

Nothing could be hidden in solid stone. A little less to search.

They turned right and came upon a row of doors on the left.

"The guests are staying in these rooms. Here's the Donkey." Ursa-bee pointed at the last door, on which an elegant donkey had been painted in yellow, with a garland of blue flowers around its neck.

When Johan-bee opened the door, Elodie thanked him twice, to make up a little for the bees' rudeness.

The room was tiny. If Johan-bee had spread his arms, his fingers would have touched each wall. The head of the bed abutted the wall next to the door and the foot touched the one opposite. Still, a bed was a luxury compared to her pallet on the floor at her parents' Potluck Farm.

Next to the foot of the bed stood a three-legged stool. A wooden chest squatted against the adjacent wall. The chamber was warm and glowworm bright.

Ursa-bee lifted the pillow to reveal a dark-blue linen mask. "Tie this on to block the light."

Elodie took off her boots. Ursa-bee and Johan-bee left. As soon as the bees had returned to the hall, she'd leave, too, and start her search.

While she waited, she'd lie down.

She was asleep as soon as her head touched the pillow.

CHAPTER TWENTY-ONE

asteress Meenore had interviewed the bees who guarded the Replica when High Brunka Marya discovered the theft. Both had been at the Oase for more than fifteen years, and they'd sworn that their post had never been abandoned. If true—and IT had found no reason to doubt them—then the most likely time for the theft was near the end of Ursa-bee and Johan-bee's turn guarding, when he'd been in the privy and she'd gone to investigate the weeping.

IT had also already interrogated Johan-bee and Ludda-bee. The conversation with the cook left IT wishing to scrub ITs earholes. Johan-bee's brief answers had revealed little. He'd talked at length only about his digestive difficulties.

IT chose Dror-bee to interview next.

"Please find the Replica, Masteress." Dror-bee looked hopeful and eager to help.

"I intend to. You are from Zertrum, are you not?"

"How did you guess?"

ITs smoke spiraled. "I never guess. You are not permitted to guard the Replica, correct?"

Dror-bee shook his head. "Yes. I've only been a bee for three months."

"Just so. Who do you think may have stolen it?"

The bee shrugged, raising his shoulders to his ears.

"Speculate."

He clapped his hands, then wrung them. "Mistress Sirka."

"Ah. Is she avaricious?"

Silence. He shifted from foot to foot.

Masteress Meenore wished to hold him in place. The man was never still. But why wouldn't he answer? Ah. "*Avaricious* means greedy."

"She doesn't mind being poor."

"Why then?"

"She's reckless."

"Mmm. How would she have done it?"

Dror-bee put his index finger on his chin, the image of someone thinking. "I don't know where it was kept, so it's hard to guess. She's a night owl. She would do it when others are sleeping."

"Mmm." How did this youth know the barber's ways—her recklessness, her tardiness to bed? "You became a bee rather than a soldier. How did that choice come about?"

"My father said I couldn't stay on our farm, and I could be only one or the other. I'm happy as a bee."

Masteress Meenore's internal flame flared. Here was a reason for anger against someone on Zertrum. "A farmer always needs more help. Why then did your father have no use for you?"

Dror-bee nodded twice. "I had too many ideas, which often failed. Father said I made him tired. Mother said, 'The sheep with too much wool gets caught in the brambles.'"

Masteress Meenore thought that Lahnt had as many proverbs as sheep. "Are you enraged at your parents for sending you away?"

"No!"

"Were you angry at the time?"

His shoulders slumped. "I was sad. But Marya doesn't mind my ideas, and a month ago when I found two lost goslings for a farmer, he thanked me. He said"—Dror-bee's chest expanded—"that Lahnt was lucky to have bees like me."

"You called Mistress Sirka reckless. Why?"

Dror-bee flung out his arms. "You'd think so, too, if you watched her cut hair. It's a wonder she hasn't chopped off an ear, and yet the result is always pleasing."

"Is it reckless of her to court a bee?"

Softly, so IT had to strain to hear, he said, "It is hope-less."

"Please tell the alleged thief to come to me. I will speak with her next."

But a reckless thief would snatch and run. If Mistress Sirka were the thief, she would have to be cunning, too. Perhaps she was.

CHAPTER TWENTY-TWO

ear and hatred had almost killed Count Jonty Um in Two Castles town. Lahnt, he thought, may finish me off. His teeth chattered, and he'd lost feeling in his feet. At a safe distance, the hunters had cleared snow and built a fire, fetching branches from the woods below, but when it was roaring, they held burning brands to keep him from approaching, until he half wished they'd thrust one at him. Fee fi! Roasting might be preferable to freezing.

He could shape-shift into a bear and have fur to warm him; however, he feared what the men would do to it or it would do to them.

Brunka Arnulf arrived at last on a mule. He jumped off, crying, "You'll kill our rescuer! Let him warm himself!"

The men backed away, and His Lordship, who was

usually graceful, lumbered to the fire. When he stopped, Brunka Arnulf flashed rainbows at his half-frozen feet.

"My rainbows have no other medicinal use, but they're good for this."

His Lordship's feet tingled agonizingly, but agony was better than no feeling at all. And being touched by rainbows made the pain worth having.

"How bad is your wound, Master Count?"

His Lordship boomed, "Not so bad for me. Dreadful for a bird. I can't fly."

Brunka Arnulf stepped back from the sound. "Otto, you chose the wrong swift to shoot. We're lucky your aim was off."

"He really is a count?" Goodman Otto said. "A *count*?"

"I believe him when he says he is."

"Oh." Goodman Otto touched his cap. "I'm s-sorry. Er . . . p-pleased to make your acquaintance. Brunka Arnulf, is it true? The Replica was stolen?"

"Alas, yes. I hear the mountain rumbling. Count Jonty Um was flying back to the Oase with information."

"I can walk, though I'll be too late."

"Then stay," Brunka Arnulf said. "Folks here need you."

His Lordship felt heat behind his eyes. Fo fum! To be needed! Meenore, he thought, if I could reach you in time, I'd leave. Forgive me for allowing myself to be wounded. Forgive me, Elodie, Nesspa. "I'll stay."

CHAPTER TWENTY-THREE

lodie awoke with no sense of how long she'd been sleeping. The glowworms shone as brightly as ever. She sat up.

Her masteress had said IT would want her in an hour or two. Had that time come? Or passed, and the Replica had been found and she had slept through it? She hoped not, then felt ashamed. Of course she wanted it to be recovered, but she preferred to be there when IT proved ITs brilliance with her *penetrating mind* helping IT reach ITs conclusions.

Most of all, she hoped His Lordship had come back.

She left the Donkey Room. Before going to the great hall, she could still investigate the other guests' rooms.

Painted on the door next to the Donkey Room was a parrot with red-and-blue plumage. She eased the door open while trying to think of an excuse in case its tenant happened to be inside.

There was no one, and no need to tarry. Albin slept here. She recognized the room as his because her favorite thing lay atop the bed: his thick book of mansioners' plays.

The cover was raised a little, and the pages didn't lie flat. He was always careless with his things. She went to the book, curious to see which play he'd marked. But when she opened it, she didn't even notice. The marker was a silver coin.

Lambs and calves! How did Albin come to have a silver, which would pay passage for all of them to and from the mainland many times over?

Did she have to mistrust him, too?

Since the room had been searched, she didn't have to replace the book exactly where it had been. Now she did comb the chamber but found nothing else of interest. Albin's satchel held only a spare undershirt. His mountain staff leaned against the chest, which proved to be empty.

Back in the corridor, the Stoat Room came next, a bigger chamber with a double bed and a single: Master Uwald and Master Robbie's quarters. Either the bees who'd searched had turned everything topsy-turvy or Master Uwald, the just-so man, was slovenly. Rich apparel was heaped on the unmade big bed, the pile capped by a single shoe, while its mate rested on the floor. Atop the chest, a backgammon game lay open. Within the chest: nothing.

By contrast, Master Robbie's bed was neatly made. At the foot, carefully folded and stacked, were three spare undershirts and two spare tunics, everything new, the undershirts silk, the tunics soft linen. The tip of something leather protruded from under the pillow. Elodie went to it and discovered a long knife in a leather sheath.

She, like everyone else, carried a little knife in her purse, for ordinary tasks that might arise, like cutting thread or opening nuts. But why a long knife? For protection? For murder? An inheritance from his grandmother?

Might it have something to do with the Replica?

As she left the room, she wondered what the bees had made of the knife. The Elk Room was Master Tuomo's. To Elodie's surprise, a lute lay across the bed. She wouldn't have guessed angry Master Tuomo to be a musician. In the distance, a clappered bell rang. She stepped out into the empty corridor and heard voices.

"Johan, wait! Don't you march off! You'd think Marya would trust me to fetch the child alone. I'd trust . . ."

No time to return to her room, but at least they hadn't caught her in anyone else's. "Has the Replica been found?" she called.

Johan-bee came into sight first, then Ludda-bee.

"No, not—"

"That dragon hasn't discovered anything. Girl, I pity you for having to travel with the meddling, sneering monster."

"IT wasn't meddlesome with me," Elodie said mildly.

The three started back toward the great hall.

"Aren't you the lucky one. But what does a child have for anyone to meddle over?"

In the great hall her masteress was interrogating Master Uwald and Master Robbie—or perhaps not. The two humans were sitting on the floor. IT had lowered ITs head and was leaning on ITs elbows. A thin stream of pink smoke rose—an irritated dragon.

"Mistress Elodie, approach, if you will."

When she drew close, she saw that IT and Master Uwald were playing Thirty-One. A smiling Master Robbie dealt the cards. Happy to be in Master Uwald's company or in ITs?

Master Robbie placed two cards faceup and one facedown in front of IT and set the same before Master Uwald.

IT brushed the cards away. "Enough. I cannot part with more books."

"Masteress," Master Uwald said, "I was unlucky once in a great affair of the heart. Since then, the cards smile on me. The dice smile on me. I believe the Replica will be found. If not"—he winked—"I can sell your books." His face became serious. "I hope it's found, for Tuomo's sake and the sake of his sons and of our poor workers."

Serious, Elodie thought, but not anxious.

IT straightened. "Mistress Elodie, come with me. I require your assistance with the dog. Master Robbie, you may be helpful as well. May he accompany us, Master Uwald?"

"Robbie, do you want to—"

"Yes!"

"Go then. Wrap your cloak tight around you."

A late-afternoon sun hung low in the cloudless sky. The air sparkled with cold. Followed by Masteress Meenore, Master Robbie and Elodie walked down the dragon-wide pathway IT had forged earlier. But the stairway, which IT must have hopped over, was still heaped with snow.

"Move aside." IT thrust out ITs snout and flamed. The snow vanished; the steps steamed; Master Robbie held the mourning beads and grinned.

Another of the surprising comforts his grandmother had predicted, Elodie thought, and was glad.

IT spread ITs wings and skimmed over the steps, landing lightly below.

Elodie ran down. "Masteress, let Master Robbie stand under your wings. Please!"

"We may not dally, Lodie."

IT set off at ITs slow pace, wings out. Elodie knew ITs

wings were ITs only vanity—and all IT had to be vain about. She waved for Master Robbie to hurry.

He caught up and ran under, craning his neck to see. "Whales and porpoises!"

ITs wings were crisscrossed with sinews, like the stitch lines in a quilt, between which stretched skin that was utterly different from the wrinkled brown of ITs belly. This skin was thin as a butterfly's wing and tinted the tones inside a seashell. The blue sky blended through, turning pink skin to violet, yellow to green, and pale blue to deep. From above, when Elodie was on ITs back, the hues changed constantly, depending on what they flew over.

"I wish Grandmother could see."

They continued toward the stable. Elodie hoped for a sign that His Lordship had returned, but she saw nothing and heard only Nesspa barking. As soon as they entered, he greeted her joyously and Master Robbie almost as happily. He gave IT a wide berth. The other beasts moved uneasily in their stalls.

IT settled on ITs belly in the space near the door. "Lodie . . ."

Elodie noticed IT wasn't pretending to hardly know her. She sat on the stool she'd occupied earlier. "Yes, Masteress. Masteress, shouldn't His Lordship be back by now?" Nesspa curled up on the floor at her feet.

"When he arrives, he will be here."

Master Robbie took the other stool.

"Masteress! Tell Master Robbie I'm your assistant."

"Indeed. I pay her a salary, which I will curtail if she does not begin to earn it by deducing and inducing and using her common sense. I expect you to do the same, Master Robbie, although I will not remunerate you." *Enh enh enh.*

Elodie deduced that IT didn't suspect Master Robbie of the theft.

He tilted his head, looking puzzled. "What are deducing and inducing, Masteress?"

"Lodie?"

These were the foundations of detecting. "To deduce is to reason from something you already know or from a principle."

IT nodded ITs huge head.

"To induce is to pull the truth from facts, from what you saw or heard or smelled."

"*Pull* is inelegant, Lodie. Now, describe where the Replica was concealed. I have had an account from Ursa-bee and I must compare."

She did, hoping she was including more details than the bee had.

"Ah. Ursa-bee neglected to mention a storage room.

Repeat, Lodie: the door to it from the corridor was kept locked?"

"Yes. High Brunka Marya said she has the only key."

"The lock is locked on both sides of the door?"

"No, Masteress. Only on the corridor side."

"Careless! Of a piece with everything else. So the storage room door in her chamber entirely lacks a lock?"

Elodie nodded.

"Master Robbie, earlier you alluded to a handkerchief that weeps. Pray tell, what is this?"

He wet his lips. "Masteress . . ." He repeated, clearly enjoying the word, "Masteress, it's one of four enchanted things, but the handkerchief is the only one that's missing." He described the others, ending with "Mistress Elodie can make a person laugh as well as the flower can."

"It is a shame Lodie could not hear the handkerchief and model it. You were told this weeping can insinuate itself inside one's mind?"

Master Robbie nodded. "Yes, Masteress."

Elodie wondered if she could mansion the handkerchief even without having heard it. She closed her eyes, summoning sadness. The flower had started laughing slowly, and the nightingale had chirped before it sang. She sighed deeply, looking at the stable floor, and thought of the people who might die on Zertrum. Her eyes filled. She looked at her masteress and brought His Lordship to mind. A sob bubbled up. She looked at Master Robbie. He'd lost one home and might soon lose another. A tear trickled down her cheek.

The sadness took her. She wiped her streaming eyes and nose with her sleeve and sobbed and wept.

CHAPTER TWENTY-FOUR

"Mistress Elodie, don't . . ."

Even IT touched her arm. "Lodie . . ."

Now she had to make her sadness anyone's sorrow, so it would enter their minds, too. She raised the pitch of her wailing until it became a knife tip of misery, as inescapable as loss and disappointment and sickness and death.

Master Robbie held his hands over his ears and turned away from them, his shoulders shaking. ITs smoke darkened to gray-black, the darkest Elodie had ever seen it. ITs emerald eyes glittered, and a drop of clear liquid fell from one of ITs overhanging fangs.

She fought for composure. Her weeping diminished gradually, as the flower's laughter had. The unhappy thoughts receded. She could breathe deeply again and look around.

"Astonishing, Elodie. An accomplishment."

"You did it on purpose?" Master Robbie's question was half accusation.

She nodded. It was a performance she didn't want to repeat.

"You proved the truth of Ursa-bee's account. A harder heart than hers would have found that weeping irresistible. Even I, a dry and leathery creature, could not resist reaching out to comfort you. And if you had not been visible before us, I would have been hard put to locate the source of the sound."

"Really?"

Master Robbie seemed to have recovered. "You're truly a mansioner."

Of course she was. But she savored the praise.

IT, however, never lingered on others' achievements. "What else did you discover?"

"Master Robbie told me about the guests and the barber and the bees. He said Mistress Sirka—"

"Permit him to speak for himself."

Master Robbie retold his information with relish. Under ITs questioning, he divulged more than he had to Elodie. He recalled details about several other bees. One hummed constantly under his breath. Another always smelled of mint. He reported which was the Oase's spinner, which the weaver, which ones made soap. He ended by saying, "Deeter-bee is the historian, and he can tell you anything about Lahnt."

"You are Master Uwald's ward, are you not?"

Master Robbie looked startled, but he nodded.

"And this arrangement is not of long standing?"

Master Robbie's hands found the mourning beads. "Just since my grandmother died two weeks ago." He paused. "But I always knew he would come. If he died before she did, Master Tuomo was to be my guardian. As soon as I was old enough to understand, Grandmother told me I was going to inherit Nockess Farm."

Elodie clenched her teeth to keep her jaw from falling open. Yet he'd lived in poverty! How strange! He'd been poor with a cloud of wealth hanging over his head, and only tragedy would bring the rain of coins. Couldn't they have arranged it better?

ITs eyebrow ridges furrowed. "Your parents and your grandfather are all dead?"

Master Robbie let the mourning beads go. "Mother and Father died of fever when I was three. Grandfather was a fisherman. Grandmother said he wanted to be rich like Master Uwald, but he died before I was born."

Elodie's throat tightened in pity.

Masteress Meenore showed no sympathy. "Had you

encountered either Master Uwald or Master Tuomo before your grandmother's demise?"

Master Robbie looked confused. "Her death, Masteress?"

"So I said."

"No, Masteress. I never met them before."

Likely that's why he has the knife, Elodie thought. To protect himself from these strangers. She had a sudden idea. "Has High Brunka Marya offered you asylum?"

Master Robbie said yes.

"Are you going to stay?" Elodie leaned forward. "Do you want to be a bee?"

He shook his head sharply. "I won't be a bee."

Elodie felt relief. Bees led limited lives, as she saw it. And they couldn't marry, although that thought came and went so quickly, she hardly noticed it.

"But I may stay. I haven't decided."

"Master Robbie, is Master Uwald aware of this offer of refuge?"

"I don't think so, Masteress."

"High Brunka Marya is a veritable pied piper to lure away a child. It is pernicious, this brunka habit of deciding what is best for everyone." IT blew a puff of pink smoke. "Lodie, did you think to ask Master Robbie about asylum because the same had been proposed to you?"

She nodded. "From my parents and you."

The pink darkened to an outraged red. "She would deprive you of *me*?"

Master Robbie blinked in surprise, then smiled.

Elodie seized the opportunity. "She must have noticed that you often mistreat me by calling me *Lodie,* though my name is Elodie." Nervously, she added, *"*Enh enh enh."

ITs smoke whitened. *Enh enh enh.* "And why refuge from your parents?"

She explained.

"Mmm." IT returned to Master Robbie. "Do you suppose Nockess Farm would still be yours should you remain here?" IT was thinking aloud. "Who would own the farm if you became a bee?"

"I'm not going to be—"

"Answer my question."

"Maybe the brunkas. Maybe Master Tuomo."

"Presumably Master Tuomo has known for years that he will not inherit Nockess Farm. Can you confirm that, Master Robbie?"

"No one said."

"Is he pleasant to you?"

"He doesn't seem angry. He was often angry at his horse on our way here. He kicked it and used the whip, but he was kind to me in a gruff way."

"Mmm. He may not have made his true ire known. Expecting events to happen—your grandmother's death,

143

your becoming Master Uwald's ward—and the events' occurrence differ vastly. One may think oneself reconciled and find oneself enraged instead. If it were not that Master Tuomo's sons are on Zertrum, he would be my favorite suspect."

"But he didn't know where the Replica was kept," Elodie said.

"He may have. Many others did: all the brunkas as well as the bees presently living here and those who formerly did. Knowledge may be bought. Even a brunka may have a price."

Master Uwald might have bought the information, too, Elodie thought, but he'd lose his farm. "What did Goodwife Lilli say about Master Uwald?"

IT said, "Her name was Lilli?"

Master Robbie nodded.

"After the flower, the roots of which I have often enjoyed roasted and salted. Did Goodwife Lilli prepare you for the day that has now arrived?"

"She hadn't seen him in many years. She said he had been a kind *boy*." He grinned. "A boy! Not tall and strapping such as she preferred—she laughed when she said that. But she didn't say much. Grandmother didn't like to talk about the past."

"Did she tell you how to comport yourself as a rich boy?"

He laughed. "She said I should never miss the chance to kick a servant down the stairs. I should insist that tasks be done in half the time required. She made me practice wagging my finger and raising my eyebrows." He demonstrated.

Enh enh enh.

Elodie smiled although she felt sad.

"She said Master Uwald—my guardian . . ." He turned to Elodie and shrugged. "I don't know what to call him."

She wanted to pat his shoulder but contented herself with looking sympathetic.

"How does he wish to be called?"

"Granduncle or just Grand, Masteress, but it feels strange."

Grand by itself sounded grandiose to Elodie.

"He's not my uncle." Master Robbie spoke with his head down, squeezing his hands together. "He says he lo— cares about me, says he has ever since Grandmother wrote to him to tell him that my parents had died and I existed."

"Nine years," IT said, "if she wrote soon after their deaths. Enough time for affection to swell. Whether Master Uwald's feeling is true or imagined will be proven in time."

Elodie found this dry logic comforting.

Master Robbie raised his head. "Grandmother said Granduncle might be better than most rich people, but he was still a dicer and a wagerer."

145

"Do you agree?" IT leaned in toward Master Robbie, ITs flat eyes a deeper green than usual. "Is he better?"

"I guess so. He never mistreated his horse. Soon after we came here, he told Ludda-bee and Dror-bee not to tease Johan-bee. They didn't listen, but it was kind of him to try. And he's been talking to Johan-bee. I think he's helping him learn to speak up and teaching him backgammon."

"He has true sympathy," Elodie said.

IT sniffed.

Elodie asked, "Has he done much betting?"

"When I played queets he bet on me." Master Robbie's nose pinkened again. "He never lost."

IT snorted, and Elodie wondered how many of ITs books Master Uwald had won.

Master Robbie continued. "He wagered on anything: how soon the innkeeper would bring our meal, what the weather would be, which room the high brunka would put us in. But he didn't put money on everything. Sometimes it was more like guessing or predicting."

Elodie's attention wandered. She was impatient to tell IT about Master Uwald's messy bed and about the other rooms she'd entered, but Master Robbie's knife was one of her discoveries, and he probably wouldn't like being spied on. So, hoping to somehow escape his anger, she began indirectly. "Did the bees find anything in the guests' chambers that gave you a hint, Masteress?"

"The high brunka said nothing of import had been discovered."

"Was anything found among the bees' things?" Elodie asked.

IT twitched ITs tail. "I have not been told their possessions were gone through. Lodie, ask the high brunka about the results."

"Has anyone searched here?" Master Robbie asked.

"Two bees came before dawn. Their visit—"

"Masteress, will the bees—"

"Do not interrupt, Lodie. What is it?"

"Will the bees even recognize a clue when they see one? Wouldn't it be wonderful if someone who was trained by a masteress could search?" Elodie doubted even IT was intelligent enough to understand her hint, so she added, "In secret."

ITs smoke turned rosy. "Master Robbie, Nesspa would benefit from exercise. I am sure you can find a rope to hold him, or otherwise he may attempt to seek his master."

How quick ITs understanding is! Elodie thought proudly.

Master Robbie slid off his stool. His gaze went from IT to Elodie, and she knew he realized he was being sent away. He tied a rope to Nesspa's collar and left.

"Lodie, I hope you did not search the guests' rooms."

"I did! I thought you'd want me to."

"I? A dragon with a secret hoard? Which you had the good sense not to invade when you were alone in my lair."

She felt ashamed. "But the high brunka—"

"The high brunka informed her guests of the search, which you did not have the grace to do."

Elodie blinked back tears, but she still thought she'd been right to investigate.

ITs smoke whitened gradually. "Tell me what you discovered."

She shrugged. "Not so much."

"Do not compound your error by wasting it."

"I wouldn't even have looked in Albin's room if I had known it was his. I found a silver. A silver!"

"If you were determined to pry, you were correct to pry everywhere."

"He shouldn't have a silver!"

"I will keep his wealth in mind. It is suggestive, but he may have obtained the coin quite recently and reasonably. You must ask him."

"But he'll know how I know." And feel hurt.

"Injured feelings are of no concern to us. We will not be able to evaluate the significance of the silver until we understand how he came by it. Come, Lodie. He is your friend. If he is innocent, I suppose you would like him to continue in that capacity."

"I trusted him!"

ITs tone softened. "Perhaps you still may. His answer will reveal whether or not you can. What else?"

"Master Uwald, for all his just-so looks, scatters his things hither and yon. He is beyond untidy. Master Robbie, the reverse. His bed was neatly made."

"Master Robbie is unaccustomed to servants."

She whispered, "Master Robbie keeps a long knife under his pillow."

"He feels endangered. I pity him. I suggest you confess to Master Robbie, too."

"I can't!"

"I am embarrassed for you."

She swallowed hard.

"You must. Of all the humans here, I have determined he alone merits our trust. We should deserve his."

She nodded, dreading his return.

"What else did you find?"

"Master Tuomo's chamber was in order. He plays the lute."

"Did you hear him play it?"

"No, but he brought it with him."

"Likely he plays it, but assume nothing."

"Yes, Masteress."

Master Robbie returned with Nesspa. "He ate snow!"

The dog nuzzled Elodie, making her skirt wet. She felt

undeserving of even his affection. He trotted off toward the back of the stable.

"Lodie?"

She confessed to Master Robbie, although she didn't mention the knife, just that she'd been in their chamber.

His lips formed a thin, angry line. He looked away from her and said nothing.

She wished she knew what he was thinking.

"Mistress Sirka's room, Lodie?"

"I didn't have time to go in."

"I've been there." Master Robbie took his place on the stool again. He still avoided Elodie's eyes.

They waited expectantly.

"She and I played queets in the great hall. Granduncle staked me with three coppers, and I won every game. I saw she hated to give me her coins, and I wanted to see a barber-surgeon's tools, so she paid me by showing me."

How kind of him, Elodie thought.

"If not for Nockess Farm, I'd want to be a barber-surgeon. A barber-surgeon travels. He takes people's pain away." He met Elodie's eyes, and his face was no longer angry.

She let out a long breath.

"Sometimes he saves their lives. Even when he just cuts hair, people look better when he's done. I still think it's the best thing to be."

Instead, he'd have to be a rich man.

IT scratched along ITs neck. "I believe fleas have made their wretched home under my scales. Master Robbie, what did you see in her chamber?"

"Her thumb-lancet has three blades. She said some have nine."

Why, Elodie wondered, would anyone need nine ways to bleed people?

"Her pelican has a polished wooden handle. The rest is iron." He pointed at a front tooth. "She showed me how she puts the claw over the tooth to pull it."

Elodie hoped never to need the dreaded pelican.

"The dragon tooth," IT said with a self-satisfied air, "is impervious to rot. Did you see anything that may have bearing on the theft?"

"I don't know. She showed me a love bolus and said she meant to drop it into Dror-bee's pottage. I don't know if she has yet."

"How curious that she announced her intention. Be so kind as to tell us what was in this pellet, if she told you. Elodie has an extensive knowledge of poisons."

Master Robbie grinned. "Really? Poisons?"

She nodded and didn't explain that anyone who lived on a farm knew the ordinary poisons, and anyone who read the mansioners' plays learned the exotic ones. Let him admire her.

He recited, "She said it contained hawthorn, southern-wood, sage, dried rose petals, and silverweed."

"Master Robbie paid attention, Lodie. Perhaps he foresaw a use for his own ends."

They both blushed.

"Common herbs," Elodie said. "Not poisonous. I don't know why they'd make a person love someone."

"Perhaps it is in the combination. She had other herbs, did she not, Master Robbie?"

"She had a sack full of little packets wrapped in burlap. She didn't say what they were."

"Keep this in mind when you return, both of you."

"You're not coming, too, Masteress?" Master Robbie asked.

IT didn't answer. "My interviews yielded little. The so-called historian was as unrevealing as a clam. See if you can get more from him. The sugary Ursa-bee and the lumpish Johan-bee admitted to leaving their posts at the same time."

"Lambs and calves!"

"Whales and porpoises!"

IT continued calmly. "Johan-bee frequently visits the privy and remains there interminably, attested to by all the bees I spoke with. Ursa-bee heard weeping, which she was unable to resist. That was likely the handkerchief you so ably mansioned, Lodie."

"Thank you."

"Johan-bee and Ursa-bee were the only two who confessed to abandoning their station, but others may have as well. Everyone was exceedingly lax, as if a theft could never occur."

"After they returned," Elodie said, "did Johan-bee and Ursa-bee look to see if the Replica was gone?"

"They did, and the Replica remained. We know then, at the very least, that at that time, the morning before the blizzard, the Replica still stood where it was supposed to—"

"Unless . . ." Master Robbie said.

Elodie stiffened.

ITs smoke reddened. "Do not interrupt me, boy."

"Beg pardon!"

"Granted. I hope you have something important to contribute."

"Unless there was a replica of the Replica that could have tricked them."

CHAPTER TWENTY-FIVE

ilence fell.

After a minute, Masteress Meenore said, "This boy has an original mind, Lodie."

Master Robbie fairly glowed.

Elodie felt a pinprick of jealousy. Which was better, she wondered, penetrating or original? "The recess in the chimney is darker than the rest of the room," Elodie conceded. "There are no glowworms in the hiding place. A person could be fooled."

IT blew green smoke, signifying dragon confusion. "A new possibility when there already are too many. Master Robbie, you have wandered the corridors of the Oase since your arrival, have you not?"

"Sometimes."

"Can you incise in the dirt a map of the corridors around

High Brunka Marya's room? Include the chambers there, and do not omit either the storage area or the garderobe to which Johan-bee was wont to retire."

Master Robbie fetched a coal brazier poker and crouched to scratch lines in the dirt of the stable floor. While he worked, Elodie strained her ears for any sound that might mean His Lordship's return.

ITs smoke grayed. "Lodie, why do you think I have no difficulty deciphering the lines of a map and yet cannot make out a single letter in a word?"

The tragedy of ITs life lay in ITs inability to read.

If they'd been alone, she'd have ventured to pet ITs leg. "I don't know, Masteress."

Master Robbie stood and backed away.

"Mmm. Fascinating. Mmm." IT was silent. "Mmm." More silence. "Listen well. If the thief, who, naturally, knew where the Replica was hidden, had merely picked the lock of the storage area—"

"Masteress—"

"Do not interrupt your betters, Lodie. What did you want to say?"

"I forgot to tell you—"

IT glared at her.

"The high brunka said the lock was made on the mainland and can't be picked."

"There is no lock that may not be picked unless a spell

has been put on it, and perhaps one was. This lock may merely be difficult to pick, a lengthy endeavor, which the thief would wish to avoid. We will theorize along other lines. Assist me in my reasoning."

Elodie knew from experience that IT wanted no assistance.

"If the Replica was an imitation, why not leave it there? But the recess was empty when you saw it, Lodie, yes?"

She nodded.

"Regrettably, you have not added anything to our deliberations, Master Robbie."

"I'm sorry. I—"

"However, I admire your ingenuity. I continue my reasoning: When Ursa-bee said she and Johan-bee had verified that the Replica was still in its place, I suspected that the thief was concealed in the chamber with the two of them, but the storage room offers an even better hiding place. Let us assume then that the theft happened on their watch, and the blizzard frustrated escape. Master Robbie, your—"

"If that's when it happened, that's good, isn't—"

"You have interrupted me again, Lodie." IT sighed elaborately. "Yes. The later the better, although the urgency has hardly diminished. Master Robbie, your request to see the Replica again brought the theft to light. We may assume that the thief, or thieves—"

"Thieves, Masteress?"

"I will get to that, Lodie. The thief—or thieves—is alarmed, and frightened people may be deadly. Be sure to tell the high brunka that. Say *deadly*."

She reminded IT, "Thieves?"

"A single thief may have done it. A pair would be more certain of success. The bees know Johan-bee's routine, and the guests and the barber-surgeon do as well, do they not, Master Robbie?"

He nodded.

"When Johan-bee has left for the privy . . . But how does the thief know the precise moment he leaves? Although Ursa-bee said he often goes shortly before the end of a watch, this would have to be timed with exactitude."

"The thief is nearby, listening?" Master Robbie suggested. "Johan-bee has a heavy step."

"And the rushes make noise when anyone but a brunka walks."

"True. The wretch places the handkerchief's box in one of these rooms, most likely this one . . ."—IT tapped a room on Master Robbie's map—"concealed in some way. The thief opens the box and touches the handkerchief. The weeping begins, but softly, allowing him or her time to exit, leaving the door a little ajar so the weeping may be heard. The villain rushes along this route"—a talon traced a path along the corridor that ran parallel to the one that led to the high brunka's room—"passes the closed door of the garderobe, turns right, then left. The way is long but achievable. He or she hastens through the high brunka's chamber into the storage room and waits for Johan-bee and Ursa-bee to come and go. The scoundrel then takes the Replica and exits through the storage room door to the corridor. If someone is in the corridor, the scheme fails. But the corridor is rarely traveled. The risk is small. The thief then retrieves the handkerchief and spirits it away, I know not where."

"Oh," Master Robbie breathed. "I can picture it."

"But," Elodie said, "if Johan-bee is quicker than usual, the villain is caught. I see why two are better." With mounting excitement, she continued. "If the thief has a partner, the first thief can put the handkerchief here"—she touched a different room—"and turn into one of these side passageways. Thief two can wait here." She pointed at the corridor IT had said the thief would have to dash through, near the turn that led to the privy. "Thief two—"

Master Robbie broke in. "Thief two has a shorter distance to travel to reach the high brunka's room. But who are they?"

IT blew gray smoke. "Everyone has a motive to steal an item that is worth a great deal. Even the already rich are not exempt; they may want more. I am at a loss."

Elodie had never heard IT say such a thing before.

"When you return, do not waste your energy searching shelves and cabinets. Let others do it, because it must be done, but these thieves are too cunning to have hidden the Replica there. Why is that? Think, Lodie! Think, Master Robbie!"

His face wore a strained look, which Elodie recognized.

Think! she thought. Prove I have an original mind, too! Ah. "Because the thieves couldn't guess where the searchers would look first. Anyone might stumble on the Replica just by luck."

"Excellent, Elodie."

Elodie!

"But . . ." Master Robbie hesitated. "If it isn't in the Oase, where is it? Outside is big."

"Indeed. I do not say the Replica is outside. It is equally likely to be in or out, but we will find it most quickly through reason. Continue to deduce and induce and use your common sense, both of you. The thieves and the hiding place are twined together. We have uncovered the method. The motive is greed."

Quoting the puppet, Elodie said, "'Expectation misleads.' Perhaps the motive isn't greed. Maybe there's another explanation." She felt silly. "Something inside the Replica? Something it can do?"

IT lifted ITself off ITs belly. "Doubtful. Lacking in common sense."

Elodie blushed.

"But there may be an additional motive: rage, for example. Dror-bee has reason to be angry at his family for sending him away. Mistress Sirka may be angry, too. Her beloved is a bee because of the family. I suspect the two of a connection before they arrived here. Neither, however, professes to know where the Replica was kept nor has the means to purchase the information. Nonetheless, they are still possible thieves."

Elodie asked, "Do we know what people did after Ursa-bee and Johan-bee's watch and before the blizzard?"

"A useful question. Ursa-bee said that she and carping Ludda-bee as well as lumpish Johan-bee, after he returned from the garderobe yet again, dug up the last of the season's beets."

Master Robbie said, "A few bees also go out every morning to feed and water the beasts in the stable. One of them milks the goats. Master Tuomo stepped out after the snow began to watch the storm."

ITs gray smoke darkened. "We have too many possible villains, including even your Albin, Lodie. I had hoped for His Lordship's information to help me reduce the number."

"Do you think something terrible has happened to him?"

IT never sweetened the truth. "I am resolved to find out. Shortly I will leave you."

Then both her friends would be in danger. Elodie

ground her teeth to keep from begging IT not to go.

"The danger to me is slight, Lodie. Fire cannot harm me, and I can rise above a rockslide. If I must, I will lift His Lordship out of danger."

Elodie suspected that IT had an exaggerated idea of ITs strength.

"My fear is more for you. You may trust Master Robbie—"

"At your service."

"Do not interrupt. You may trust him because he revealed the theft."

Master Robbie bowed from the waist, a deep bow, much more respectful than the slight obeisance he'd given Elodie.

IT continued. "You may also trust the high brunka, who cannot gain by the theft. Share our discussion with her. When I am gone, she will be the only one holding back chaos. Help her however you can."

They both nodded. IT waddled to the stable door. Master Robbie jumped out of the way of ITs tail. The two followed IT outside, where a cold day had descended into frigid darkness.

"Lodie, sleep tonight. Master Robbie as well. The thief or thieves cannot leave, and you need your faculties. Lodie, consult with Master Robbie as I have consulted with you both."

That is, not at all, Elodie thought.

Master Robbie dared to say, "You'd like her to discuss her ideas with me?"

"I would. Discuss yours with her as well. If your deducing and inducing lead you to the miscreants, apply common sense before you proceed. Master Robbie: Lodie may act hastily and without thought for consequences—in a word, recklessly. Restrain her for both our sakes."

Elodie protested. "Masteress, I'm not—"

"To their faces, you called a cruel king cruel and an enormous ogre—before you knew his kind heart—unfair. You thrust your hand into the high brunka's rainbow."

"But—"

"Farewell." IT leaped into the air; ITs wings caught the wind; IT beat ITs way north.

Elodie shivered against the loss of ITs warmth. Fly swiftly. Take care. Stay safe. Hurry back.

CHAPTER TWENTY-SIX

hese will do." His Lordship stood in boots of a sort, a rough tunic, and an equally rough hooded cloak. "Thank you."

Hours earlier, in midafternoon, Brunka Arnulf had told Goodman Otto, the hunter who'd shot the count, to ride to the nearest cottage for cloth to cover the ogre.

As soon as Goodman Otto left, the other men had departed, too, to gather their families and leave the mountain.

"Warn everyone on your way," Brunka Arnulf said before they started off. He closed his eyes. "The rumbling is louder. Leave your herds and your flocks. There isn't time."

Fee fi! The poor beasts.

"Take refuge in the caves of Svye."

Svye? His Lordship remembered, *Bear Is So Zany, No Dogs Lie.* Svye would be the mountain just south of Zertrum.

The hunters left.

"Master Count, the closest cottage belongs to Widow Fridda, who has five children. When you are no longer naked, will you help them?"

"Yes."

He gave directions to the widow's cottage. "Take them to the caves and then come back. She'll tell you who else needs aid." Brunka Arnulf mounted his mule. "Good luck. May the Replica be found." He flapped the reins and started up the mountain.

His Lordship added dry brush to the fire. Nesspa would be missing his master almost as much as his master missed him.

Count Jonty Um's shoulder wound smarted and was warm when he touched it.

The ground, which was bare of snow around the fire, felt calm and steady, but below, what agitation might there be? When would it rage so loud that humans and ogres could sense it?

Goodman Otto returned an hour later with a heap of animal skins, blankets, and long leather straps—and Widow Fridda on a donkey.

His Lordship ran behind the boulders but peeked out so he could see.

The goodman unloaded the supplies and left. The widow, a tall, solid-looking woman, clung to the neck of her donkey.

Another frightened person.

After a few silent minutes, the widow approached the boulder and threw a blanket on the ground then turned away. His Lordship wound the cloth around his waist and stepped out.

He could help no one barefoot. He picked up a skin and a strap, stepped on the skin with his left foot, and pulled it up to make a lumpy boot, which he attempted unsuccessfully to hold together by tying the strap around his ankle.

The widow recovered from her fear quicker than most. "No one can walk in that." She gestured for him to sit on a large rock.

He did and extended a foot.

She took an awl—for piercing holes in skins—out of the purse at her waist and scrutinized his foot. "Trim toenails. Maybe you really are a count."

His Lordship thought, She's speaking to me as I might to Nesspa. "Thank you."

"Oh!" She dropped the awl into her lap. "Beg pardon. I'm sure you must be a count, Your Countship. I thought you spoke only the ogre language."

There was no ogre language. Ogres spoke the tongue of wherever they lived.

In less time than he expected, crude boots were on his feet, fur side in, bulky but warm and possible to walk in. Next, Widow Fridda contrived a tunic and hooded cloak. For the tunic she merely cut a slit in a blanket for his head. For the cloak, she made a few tucks for the hood in another blanket and sewed in fabric strips for ties. While she labored, His Lordship fed the fire in his usual silence.

"There," the widow said. "Hard times make a pauper of a king."

He donned his new apparel—scratchy and smelling of smoke and tallow. "Thank you."

She folded the leftover skins. "I'll be going home now."

"Brunka Arnulf told me to help you."

"Your Countship is a bee?" She tilted her head. "There's plenty to do. Fences to be mended. Grain to be put out for the sheep. I have a salve for your shoulder."

Goodman Otto hadn't warned her about the mountain? Ah. If he had, she wouldn't have come. His Lordship explained in a few words.

She rushed to the donkey. "My babes! Come!"

He didn't move. "Do you have cats?"

She was already several yards away. "One cat. Hurry."

That was all right then. A single cat couldn't wish hard

enough to make him turn into a mouse. In two strides he caught up with her and put his hand on the donkey's rump for guidance in the deepening dusk. They traveled north and upward, their breath puffing white in a quiet, windless cold. As they went, he realized that going to Svye would have to wait for morning. He didn't know how they'd do it even then, since the widow's farm cart would instantly be mired in snow.

He wondered when he might eat again.

After a half hour, when night had fallen, they reached her home, where firelight shone through the single window. She tethered the donkey and bustled inside.

Although the hut's walls came up to his chest, the steep thatched roof made the whole structure about a foot taller than he was. The wall gave off a little heat from the fire within. He stood close enough to benefit, but his head and shoulders were in the cold, and the exertion of walking no longer warmed him.

The donkey and the widow's cart occupied a lean-to that abutted the cottage. He could haul the cart out and curl up in the shed, where the ground was free of snow. The beast wouldn't mind. They'd be company for each other.

However, he wanted the Widow Fridda's approval of this arrangement.

She emerged from the cottage with a baby in her arms

and a clay crock in her free hand. "This will ease your shoulder, Your Countship."

He crouched and bared his shoulder. She spread the ointment, which smarted and smelled like a frightened ferret.

"Are you hungry?" she asked.

"Yes."

She returned without the baby, carrying her entire pottage pot and a ladle. "Better you eat it than the volcano."

She gave him permission to sleep in the lean-to, then went back inside. He started on the pottage: no meat, many onions, thick with oatmeal, and flavored with a spice he didn't recognize and didn't like. But he finished to the last speck.

Soon he was on his side in the shed, a mound of hay for a pillow, the donkey's even breathing reminding him of Nesspa.

At least the dog was safe, and Elodie and Meenore would see that he lived well if his master never returned.

He slept.

CHAPTER TWENTY-SEVEN

tars, a quarter moon, and the gleaming snow showed Elodie and Master Robbie the path back to the Oase.

"I'm not reckless!" Elodie clutched her cloak tight around her.

"Did you really call Greedy Grenny cruel?"

"It popped out. I think ahead—usually."

"Did you, when you searched our room?" He didn't add, *And saw my knife,* but the accusation was there.

She defended herself. "I did it to find the thief."

"It had been searched by bees."

"Everybody sees something different." Hoping to win· him over, she added, "If you'd been there, you might have noticed a detail I missed."

He said nothing.

She pulled an apology out of somewhere near her toes. "I'm sorry." Then, "But I won't apologize to anyone else."

He laughed.

Feeling immensely better, she said, "Maybe to Albin."

The Oase door was just ahead.

"IT said the thief or thieves may be deadly." She thought of what had happened in Two Castles. "Desperation could make *them* reckless." She leaned her back against the door, her face inches from his. "Let's look for desperate acts."

His face, red from the cold, reddened more. "We will!"

Together, they pushed open the door. The bee who was guarding it looked at them and said nothing.

High Brunka Marya occupied her stool in the middle of the great hall. Bees were moving sleeping pallets close to the fireplaces, where the fires burned brightly. The guests clustered at the hearth across from the entrance.

Master Uwald and Albin, both smiling, hurried to Elodie and Master Robbie.

"You must be frozen!" Master Uwald untied his cloak and wrapped it around Master Robbie, who almost disappeared in it. "Come to the fire." Master Uwald led him away.

Master Robbie turned his head to look at Elodie as they went.

"My cloak is at your service, Lady El."

She shook her head. Albin could be no warmer than

she was. She blurted, "I was in your room. I saw the silver. Where did you get it? How long have you had it?" Then, "I thought it was someone else's chamber." Which explained and excused nothing.

"You're welcome in my room. I have no secrets from a fellow mansioner. I won the coin from Master Uwald yesterday afternoon."

Probably after the theft. "What did you have to bet against him?" What, she thought, that would be worth a silver?

"He wanted my book of mansioners' plays."

"I love that book!"

"Lady El, I would have given him my right arm in exchange for coin to get you. We imagined you starving in Two Castles"—he patted her cheek—"not thriving as you were."

She blinked back tears. "You didn't get my letter?"

"No letter came. Maybe it will arrive next year and we'll laugh over it."

"What game did you play with Master Uwald?"

"Dice. I think he let me win because he wanted to help us. He could have just given me the money, but that would have meant going against the wishes of the high brunka. And he loves to play. After I won, he wanted me to wager my silver against him. Come, it's too cold by the door." He took her hand and led her toward the fireplace.

"High Brunka Marya is making us all sleep in the great hall. When the Replica is found, we should mansion this scene and all the events of the Second Theft, and you can portray her."

"Shh! She's listening!"

"No matter. Who doesn't like to be a heroine?"

The heroine needed information. Elodie went to Master Robbie, who was sitting on a pallet next to Master Uwald.

"Master Robbie . . ." Elodie walked away and hoped he would follow.

She heard Master Uwald say, "Go, but not for long. You need your sleep."

When they reached High Brunka Marya, she said, "Tell me about your conversation with Masteress Meenore."

Elodie whispered, "IT isn't sure who the thief is. If not for Master Tuomo's sons, IT would suspect him above all, because Master Robbie will inherit Nockess Farm." She nodded at him. "IT says Master Tuomo could have bought the location of the Replica."

"From a bee, lamb?"

Master Robbie didn't hesitate. "Or from a brunka."

The high brunka puffed up her cheeks and let out a long sigh. "Will IT question us again tomorrow?"

Elodie explained that IT had gone to Zertrum.

"Something has befallen His Lordship? He may not

have warned Arnulf?" She gripped her stool as if she might fall off. Tiny rainbows flared from her hands.

"The trouble may not have happened until after that."

Let His Lordship be safe, Elodie thought.

The rainbows stopped, but the colors still stained the high brunka's knuckles.

Master Robbie said, "Masteress Mecnore asked us to tell you what IT learned." He explained ITs theory that a thief had been in the storage room while Ursa-bee and Johan-bee made sure the Replica was still safe.

Elodie added, "IT thinks two thieves were probably in league with each other."

"Two could be so evil?"

Elodie described the way IT supposed they did it. "Someone has the handkerchief that weeps, or has hidden it."

"Masteress Meenore said to warn you," Master Robbie said, and Elodie thought he was enjoying the importance of his information, "that the thief—or thieves—is alarmed. IT said *most alarmed* and that frightened people can be deadly."

"Deadly here in the Oase," Elodie added, in case the high brunka didn't understand.

"Deadly here," High Brunka Marya repeated in a flat voice.

Don't lose yourself in sadness, Elodie thought. We need

you! "IT wanted us to ask you if anything was discovered among the bees' things."

"Nothing, as I expected." She blew on her fingertips, and the colors faded. "Go to sleep, kidlings. I have bees searching through the night."

In a few minutes they were all bedded down, Elodie's pallet next to Albin's. Master Tuomo sat up amid his bedding, but everyone else lay flat, breathing quietly, as people do when they're still awake. A snore came from the bees' hearth.

High Brunka Marya lay on a pallet, too, hers near the Oase entrance, the coldest spot in the great hall.

Though she'd slept little in the last three days, Elodie's mind busied her with ideas and worries. How had Master Uwald arranged to lose at dice, which was all luck?

Her thoughts wandered back to the stable and her performance as a weeping handkerchief and the ideas that she summoned to bring on the sadness. Above all, she cared most about His Lordship and now IT, who had both flown into the greatest danger.

She tried to cheer herself by making up a dragon ditty:

> *There once was an IT who sang Ta da dum*
> *And searched for an ogre called Jonty Um.*
> *Because of a theft they'd flown far away;*

Their friend could hardly bear her dismay.
She wept and never got over them.

No help in poetry. She tugged her mind to Potluck Farm, where her mother and father lay in their bedroom loft, and her father's pet goat and the family cat, Belliss, curled up below by the still-warm fireplace. Comforted enough to sleep, she fell into dreams of her masteress and His Lordship floundering in a river of molten rock.

CHAPTER TWENTY-EIGHT

asteress Meenore flew above an owl that soared over the Fluce River. Both were hunting, and IT had found ITs prey. IT swooped lower, extending a talon.

The owl twisted and veered away.

IT grinned. Another swoop, another miss, and finally success. IT held the bird out, inches from ITs snout.

"Bird, if you are His Lordship, shape-shift! Now!"

The owl remained an owl. IT roasted the bird in the air and, still flying, devoured it, savoring the crunch of the bones and beak, the tickle of the feathers descending along ITs gullet.

Owl, IT thought, symbol of wisdom, how fitting that you should be conjoined with my brilliance. If only you'd known, your last emotion would have been gratitude. *Enh enh enh.*

ITs thoughts turned darker. I take my precious self into danger for an ogre I esteem but do not love and for mountain folk I do not know, most of whom I would most certainly disdain. I leave at risk the only human I care deeply for. If a crisis comes to her . . . if she is attacked . . . if she is—I will not think it—I will be leagues away. I am unlikely to return in time to recover this Replica, and I will not be paid my fee. Folly. Folly. Folly.

IT flew on.

CHAPTER TWENTY-NINE

n the widow's shed, halfway between midnight and dawn, the donkey brayed. His Lordship raised his head, and then—fee fi!—he felt, from deep in the earth, a menacing rumble.

He touched the donkey's flank to quiet her and slipped into an uneasy sleep.

When the sky had just begun to lighten, something tickled his ankle. He opened his eyes to see a child of perhaps three years staring at his booted feet, which stuck straight up and were almost as tall as she was.

The ominous rumbling from below had gained strength. He sat up slowly, as if a fast movement might make it worse. "Good morning."

The girl covered her ears but didn't budge.

He bared his shoulder to see his wound. The cut was

still red, but the swelling had flattened. Whatever was in Widow Fridda's salve had worked a little miracle. He could fly again as a swift and bring what he'd learned to Meenore and Elodie—and be reunited with Nesspa.

The child touched the boot toe and jumped back.

What would amuse her? He lifted his right foot a few inches and let it fall hard.

She experimented by touching again.

Instantly, he raised the foot and let it drop.

She giggled and walked along his leg and touched his knee under his cloak.

He raised his whole leg and let it drop and grunted.

She laughed and sat at his side.

He smiled, pleased with himself. He touched his nose and, as softly as he could, made a honking sound, which caused the donkey to bray and the child to laugh harder.

Another girlchild, this one seeming only a little younger than Elodie, leaned on a single crutch and watched solemnly from a few feet beyond the lean-to. Her right leg twisted at the ankle, as if it had once been broken and hadn't been set properly.

When His Lordship's eyes met hers, she said, "Mother says you're a nice ogre."

How ridiculous, he thought, that *nice ogre* can almost make me weep.

"Mother says you should get ready."

He stood and would have been ready if he was going with them. Before he shape-shifted, he wanted to thank Widow Fridda for the food and the salve.

Twins, more girls, these about five years old, burst out of the house. One held a loaf of bread in both hands, and the other staggered under the weight of half a wheel of yellow cheese.

The one with the bread thrust it out. "For the good ogre."

The other extended the cheese and echoed, "For the good ogre."

He looked behind him. "Where is that good ogre?"

The twins laughed. The older girl smiled.

The twin with the bread, who seemed to be the bolder one, said, "It's you! There isn't another ogre."

"Oh. I thought there was." He took the food but felt he had no right to eat, since he'd be deserting them.

The same twin added, "Mother said the mountain is telling us to go away for a little while. I feel it talking, but I don't see how she can understand the words."

They wouldn't all be able to get down the mountain without him. The donkey wasn't big enough or strong enough to carry them, and the cart would be useless in this snow. In the growing light he scanned the landscape.

The cottage backed against the mountain. Above was snow and boulders. A half mile below, a forest grew, evergreens mixed with bare branches—no other cottages, no aid in sight.

The baby's cry blared from the hut, then stopped.

If he flew to the Oase, his knowledge might provide the clue that led to the Replica. Or the mystery would remain a mystery and these people would die.

Widow Fridda emerged from the cottage with the baby in a sling across her chest and satchels in each hand. "You didn't eat."

He bit into the bread, devoured it quickly, watched intently by four pairs of eyes, and started on the cheese. The widow hung the sacks across the donkey's back.

His Lordship swallowed. "Don't. I'll shape-shift into a draft horse and carry everyone and the satchels. The donkey can come, too, but she may run off."

"You can be a horse?" the oldest girl said.

"A docile one. A true horse, however. If you talk to me, I won't understand the words. But if there's danger, I'll wake up inside the horse." He finished the cheese. "Widow Fridda, please go inside with the children. I have to take off these clothes or I'll rip them. Please bring them with us."

"Hurry, children."

He stripped, folded his new things neatly, and began to shape-shift. The donkey brayed once and fell silent. A minute later, a large piebald horse waited outside the cottage, the ogre's intelligence fading from his eyes.

CHAPTER THIRTY

asteress Meenore spied in the distance, black against the gray dawn, the peak of Zertrum Mountain, which resembled a gaping fish.

IT thought, I am a prodigious, fleet flyer. And I am an authority on pyrology, the principles and attributes of fire. Invisible to the human eye—possibly even to the brunka eye—a film of heat shimmers above the peak: the mountain prepares to spew.

IT urged ITs wings to greater speed.

CHAPTER THIRTY-ONE

lodie slept through breakfast, although the table hadn't yet been taken down when she awoke. First she needed the garderobe. Not thinking, she headed for the corridor door from the great hall, which Dror-bee was guarding. "Stop! No one can leave." Ardent as ever, he repeated, "Stop!"

"But I came after the theft."

Dror-bee asked High Brunka Marya to rule.

"Apologies, lamb. I can't let you go alone and no one else." She appointed Ludda-bee and Johan-bee to conduct Elodie to the privy.

Elodie wondered if the high brunka paired the two to push Johan-bee to stand up for himself, or if it was a kindness to send him, because he'd be able to use the garderobe himself. Outside the great hall, she asked to be led to the privy closest to where the Replica was kept.

Ludda-bee complained about the extra distance, but she didn't say no.

As they walked, Elodie was aware that the thief had come this way. When they neared the turn into the high brunka's corridor, she thought, If the villain had an accomplice, he or she might have slipped into one of these rooms. High Brunka Marya said they were all unoccupied now. On Master Robbie's map IT had pointed at this room on her left, the Ferret Room. She decided to *ferret* about in there and wished she could tell IT the pun. Enh enh enh.

"Can I look in here?" Without waiting for an answer, she went in.

"You think the Replica may be there?" Ludda-bee asked, following her in.

"I just want to see something."

Johan-bee stayed in the doorway. Inside, there was hardly enough space for two. The cook reeked of animal fat and garlic. This chamber was narrower than Elodie's own Donkey Room, but it still held a bed, a chest, and a stool. If the box had been hidden in here, the thief would have put it where Ursa-bee wouldn't see.

No use looking in the chest, because if the handkerchief had been in there, the lid would have muffled the weeping. The floor seemed evenly strewn with floor rushes, but—she peered under the bed—had the rushes been disturbed there?

Ludda-bee grunted and crouched, too.

Too dark to tell, where there were no glowworms. Elodie tried to pull the bed out of the way as far as it would go, but it was too heavy.

"Help the girl, you inconsiderate oaf."

Ludda-bee and Elodie had to leave the room so Johan-bee could work. He pulled the bed out. From the doorway, Elodie saw rushes with no sign they'd been disturbed, except where Johan-bee had moved the legs.

They left the Ferret Room. Ludda-bee and Johan-bee turned into the corridor where the high brunka's chamber was.

Elodie stood still. If she didn't turn but continued a few steps, she'd come to a room between the high brunka's corridor and the next, where the thief might have waited if he or she had worked alone. "I want to look in this room, too, if you don't mind." She opened the door to the Turtle Room, which proved to be another tiny chamber similarly furnished.

Johan-bee went in first this time and moved the bed.

"Thank you."

Near the wall, the rushes lay too flat. A narrow, cleared path led to the flattened place that could have been made by an arm.

"Oh!" Elodie's heart speeded up. The thief had been here, had breathed this air, had opened the box, had touched the handkerchief that weeps, had hurried out. A single thief, since this was the room—if ITs theory was right.

"What do you see?" Ludda-bee bent down, too. "Nothing's there. Just rushes."

Johan-bee said, "In winter the Oase is overrun by mice."

A mouse could have caused the path and could have lain there, matting the rushes.

"He knows about mice," Ludda-bee said, starting down the corridor after Johan-bee. "A few nights ago he woke us all with his screaming when one walked across his face. You have a visage beloved by rodents, Johan."

Make a jest of it, Johan-bee! Elodie thought. He could say that all creatures loved his face. Then Ludda-bee's wit would be outwitted.

But he marched ahead of them.

Elodie called, "Thank you, Johan-bee, for your labor."

He turned. "I don't mind. Bees help." The toothache medicine almost disappeared in his smile.

They continued on to the garderobe, where Elodie disliked having people waiting for her. Again, she pitied Johan-bee.

When she came out, Ludda-bee said, "I suppose you want to use it, too, Johan."

He did. While they waited, Elodie tried to think of useful questions to ask the cook, who began a new tirade with "See how slow he is, girl? I would have finished twice by now. He's slow in everything. He took forever to dig up the beets before the blizzard, before you and the monster came. If he were cook we'd never eat. It's a wonder Master Uwald has taken an interest in him. That man is goodness itself, to poor Master Robbie, too." But, incapable of paying a complete compliment, she added, "Of course, Master Uwald will wager with anyone. He'd play dice with a pig if it had hands."

"Do you think the high brunka will find the Replica in time?"

"I do not. Marya hates to think ill of anyone. . . ."

And you love to, Elodie thought.

". . . but she'll find it in the end, and then I pity the thief."

"Who do you think might have done it?"

"Master Tuomo or Mistress Sirka. He's high and mighty, and she's low and mighty. He's losing his inheritance to Master Robbie, and she's as poor as a termite."

Johan-bee emerged at last.

Elodie thought she'd learned one thing worth knowing: there had been a single thief, if her masteress's theories were right.

As they walked the long corridor back to the great hall,

she wondered if Ludda-bee could be the thief. The cook had studied Johan-bee's habits, so she'd be aware of when he'd go to the garderobe. And she knew the Replica's hiding place. But if she took it, she'd have to leave the Oase and stop complaining. The loss would be too great.

CHAPTER THIRTY-TWO

he piebald horse picked his way down the mountain, slowed by the deep snow. He felt the low rumble far beneath his hooves, but his nature was placid and he experienced no fear.

The widow, who had never ridden a horse before, wound her fingers tight in his mane. At first the children expressed wonder at being so high up, but within a half hour they fell silent, the steady motion putting them all in a kind of trance. The baby slept. The donkey trailed behind.

An hour passed. The air warmed. The snow, which in the cold had been light as sifted flour, grew heavy and wet and harder to push through.

They entered the woods below the cottage. Although less snow had reached the ground, the trees grew close together, and the ground was stony. The horse had to pick his way and progressed more slowly. They hadn't gone far before the earth shuddered, instantly awakening the ogre in the horse. Fee fi! He stopped because that seemed safest, since every step would be treacherous, but the donkey bolted. The baby and the three-year-old wailed.

The shuddering was noiseless, but a *crack* split the air ahead as a tree toppled and narrowly missed the donkey, who surged ahead.

A great groaning and whirring came from above them on the mountain. His Lordship guessed rocks and snow were skidding down. Fo fum! Let the slide not reach them!

It didn't, but, in the distance, someone screamed.

His Lordship knew he couldn't investigate the cry, not with as many as he could carry already on board. He wished he could.

The widow whispered into his neck, "Thank you."

But she gave him too much credit. He knew they'd merely been lucky. In his mind he became a horse again and continued the slow, careful descent.

CHAPTER THIRTY-THREE

hen they delivered Elodie to the great hall, Ludda-bee went to the kitchen, and Johan-bee relieved one of the bees guarding the kitchen doorway. The breakfast table had been taken down. Hungry as she was, Elodie put thoughts of a meal out of her mind. The guests were again in their pairs, searching the shelves and cabinets that lined the walls: Master Uwald with Albin, Master Tuomo with Mistress Sirka. Master Robbie stood with Master Uwald and Albin along the north wall, but his eyes were on the door Elodie entered through. She wondered if he'd been watching for her.

Dror-bee now explored the books and relics with Ursa-bee. High Brunka Marya sat alone on her stool, watching this pair and then that and certainly listening to everyone.

Where is my masteress by now? Elodie wondered.

She jerked her head in a signal to Master Robbie, and he followed her to the high brunka.

"High Brunka—"

"Good morning, kidlings." She smiled wanly at them.

Elodie saw faint colors on her fingertips again.

"Lamb, I wish you'd come to the Oase at a more pleasant time, and we could have shown you the Replica and taken you around."

"I don't mind," Elodie said, because she could think of nothing better. "Remember when we said IT thinks there were two thieves? IT may be wrong." She explained that the rushes had been disturbed in the Turtle Room. "That's the room IT thinks would have been used if there was just one thief. But the Turtle could also be the wrong chamber. Johan-bee said there are mice, and they could have shuffled the rushes."

"He's right. We need cats, but they don't like being confined in here."

Master Robbie asked, "Are bees still searching the relics rooms?"

"They are." The high brunka sighed. "I wish we had collected fewer things." Her weak smile flickered again.

They left her.

Master Robbie said, "IT said we should ask Deeter-bee about the last theft."

The historian sat on his bench by the south fireplace, where Elodie had first seen him.

Master Robbie took Elodie's hand as they crossed the room. She felt herself blush and wondered if Albin was watching but didn't want to turn her head to see.

"I told Grand— er, Master Uwald that I'd like to be a barber-surgeon."

"What did he say?"

"He laughed. Whales and porpoises, he laughed a long time. Then he said, 'The richest boy on Lahnt wants to be a barber.' He also said we could talk more about it after this was over."

Deeter-bee watched them come.

Elodie and Master Robbie sat on the bench with him, Elodie on his left, Master Robbie on his right. Both leaned forward so they could see each other, too.

Elodie cast about for something to say. "Er . . . um . . . in one of the mansioners' plays, King Tantalus says . . ." She made her voice deep and ringing. "'History points a bloody finger at the future.'"

Not just High Brunka Marya turned to look at her; so did everyone else.

She lowered her voice. "Deeter-bee, does history point at this thief?"

He yawned. "History's finger points backward."

She persisted. "Is there anything we can learn from the other theft?"

"Who was the thief back then?" Master Robbie asked.

Deeter-bee cleared his throat. "His name is unimportant. People think only a poor person would be tempted to steal, but he was a prosperous fisherman in Zee."

Expectation misleads, Elodie thought, remembering the puppet's words.

Master Robbie frowned. "Zee?"

Deeter-bee looked him up and down. "You live in Zee?"

He touched the beads. "I used to."

"Zee isn't proud of him. He was prosperous and angry, a dangerous combination."

Elodie thought, Master Tuomo is prosperous and furious. My masteress says Mistress Sirka may be angry, but she's poor. Master Uwald is rich but not angry.

"Why was he angry?" Master Robbie asked.

"He asked the high brunka for a loan to buy a third boat, but the high brunka—not Marya back then—said two boats were enough for anyone."

Albin was also refused money by the high brunka, Elodie remembered.

"The last thief didn't want anyone killed. History will be kinder to him after this theft. He kept the Replica only a day before confessing, so that no one would suffer. He died in the earl's prison." He paused. "I will venture an opinion: This thief has a stony heart and will not confess."

Elodie wondered about the hardness of the historian's heart. Did he have a reason to be angry? Had the high brunka denied him anything? "Do you know where the Replica was kept?"

He closed his eyes. "Certainly I do."

CHAPTER THIRTY-FOUR

ll seven chambers of Masteress Meenore's heart expanded as IT took in Zertrum's beauty: peak of striated rock; mountain bones thrusting up through silver ice; snow-dusted evergreen slopes; cascading streams; the brown dot of a dwelling here and there.

Suddenly, as if a huge, invisible hand were at work, the entire mountain trembled and then became motionless again. The volcano showing its power.

IT flew close to the ground, enjoying the sight of ITs own shadow, passing over people fleeing their homes, who looked up with terrified faces.

Many drove their beasts before them. Fools! IT thought. They should have abandoned their herds and made as much haste as they could.

IT overflew a forest interrupted by a half-frozen stream.

Below, but not in ITs shadow, and so having no reason to look up, a woman and a brood of children crossed the water on the back of an enormous horse, which was followed by an unburdened donkey. IT thought, How fortunate these people are to have such a powerful and obliging mount.

Your Lordship, where have you gone? Did you shape-shift? What beast are you now?

IT continued winging ITs way north.

CHAPTER THIRTY-FIVE

fter they left Deeter-bee, Elodie whispered to Master Robbie, "Master Tuomo is angry and prosperous."

"He whipped his horse."

And he'd been her masteress's favorite suspect, if not for his sons.

Without further discussion, they went to him. Side by side, they sat on the floor and began going through the lower shelf of the same open cabinet that he was investigating.

Mistress Sirka merely stood at Master Tuomo's elbow, watching Dror-bee. Elodie followed her gaze. Dror-bee seemed completely absorbed in his task, absurdly so. If he picked up a box, it wasn't sufficient to peer inside; he had to turn it upside down as well. If everyone else were as slow as he, Zertrum would spew before much searching had been done.

And yet he appeared one of the most distressed, which might be a clue that he was mansioning his suffering. Or it might just be his character: a silly man, who heedlessly threw himself into every endeavor.

In contrast to Dror-bee, Master Tuomo's movements were quick and determined as he pulled thick tomes out of a shelf of chained books, each volume big enough to conceal the Replica if the pages had been hollowed out. Accordingly, he opened every one and thumbed through it. Before returning each book, he peered into the darkness of the shelf behind it.

Elodie said, "If the Replica had been chained, it might not have been stolen, don't you think, Master Tuomo?"

He just grunted.

Together, Elodie and Master Robbie moved relics off the bottom shelf onto the floor, so they couldn't miss anything: a heavy granite rock, sanded smooth; a wooden carving of a deer; a cottage made of clay, too small to hold the Replica; a bowl full of glass baubles.

The last relic was a wooden box, also not big enough for the Replica but certainly large enough for—

Elodie and Master Robbie looked at each other. She nodded at him, and he lifted the lid.

Gray feathers, not the handkerchief that wept. She

touched the heap, half expecting it to turn into a bird, but nothing happened.

Masteress, Elodie thought, I have no more idea of who the thieves are than you did when you left, no more idea, really, than if we'd never come to the Oase.

Master Robbie ran his hand along the shelf. "Nothing."

Elodie pointed up at Master Tuomo and shrugged, meaning they hadn't learned anything about him.

Master Robbie nodded, picking up an ancient-looking clay crock. He said, louder than if he had been speaking to just her, "I once stole a jar of honey from the inn where Grandmother worked."

Elodie felt a new stillness from Master Tuomo.

Master Robbie chuckled. "I ate a spoonful every day till it was gone."

"Did anyone catch you?" Elodie asked, as she deduced he wanted her to.

"A month later, Grandmother found the jar. She insisted that I pick my own punishment."

"I would have taken the rod to you." Master Tuomo crouched to talk to them.

"What punishment did you pick?" Elodie moved the relics back onto their shelf.

"I apologized to the innkeeper."

"That was enough for your grandmother?" Master Tuomo's voice was disapproving.

"She said it was perfect."

"What did the innkeeper do?" Elodie asked.

"He took the rod to me."

She wasn't sure the punishment had been perfect. Did it have to be so harsh?

Master Tuomo barked a sharp laugh and stood. "You're better for it. My sons are fine young men because of the rod." He returned to examining the books.

Elodie thought, How much do you truly care about your children? Might you steal the Replica and not worry about their safety?

Bees entered the great hall, the ones whom the high brunka had trusted to search the chambers. Elodie's belly hoped they were coming for the midday meal.

An idea stunned her. What if Master Tuomo had told his sons to leave Zertrum after he had departed with Master Uwald? Masteress, did you think of this? His alarm might be nothing but pretense. When she'd first learned to mansion, Albin had taught her to feign fright and anger before letting her attempt anything else. There had been nothing to it.

Ludda-bee, holding a wooden spoon, entered the great hall. Another bee trailed behind her.

High Brunka Marya clapped her hands. "Come, everyone, the entire swarm of you. You, too, you herd of guests."

Had she deduced where the Replica was?

Master Tuomo led Master Robbie and Elodie. Mistress Sirka followed more slowly. At the high brunka's stool, the bees, except those guarding the doors, had already gathered. Master Uwald and Albin approached from across the room to stand with Elodie and Master Robbie.

"Dears," High Brunka Marya began, "I've decided. I cannot apologize because this is right."

"Apologize for what?" Master Tuomo sounded angry already.

"The thief or thieves—Masteress Meenore believes there may be two—is thinking . . ." Her soft voice hardened. "You . . . Thief, thieves, I'm addressing you. You are thinking that after Zertrum explodes, the danger will be over for you. You expect I'll give up and let everyone go."

"I'll never give up," Master Tuomo said.

Albin frowned. "None of us will."

"Good. Then you won't mind that no one will leave the Oase until the Replica is found and the thieves revealed, no matter how long it takes."

"Preposterous!" burst from Master Tuomo.

"Reasonable, and as certain as snow in the mountains." She waved the bees at the entrance away from it and jerked her arm. A rainbow arched from her hand to the entrance and sealed the door in many-colored light. The rainbow dissolved, but the door rainbow glow remained.

Elodie remembered how the rainbow had stung her

hand. She doubted she could thrust her whole body through.

"Marya!" Ludda-bee cried. "We won't live even a month without provisions."

"Outside bees will bring us food. I'll let them in and out. I'll stay with you, because"—High Brunka Marya's voice faltered—"I deserve to suffer as much as anyone."

Elodie thought, I came after the theft. How can I be a mansioner or a dragon's assistant from prison? It isn't fair to treat everyone the same.

Mistress Sirka chuckled. "Not suffering for all of us."

"I make an exception only for the kidlings." The high brunka smiled a tight smile at Elodie and Master Robbie. "They may leave with the first bees to bring provisions. The rest of us are prisoners of the Oase. I may fail to find the Replica in time—a great defeat. But I will not fail to punish the thief, even if we have to die here."

CHAPTER THIRTY-SIX

y noon a tired Masteress Meenore reached the stone house with the two chimneys and found it uninhabited. IT rose into the air again, seeking a brunka who could be anywhere or an ogre who could be anywhere and any beast.

CHAPTER THIRTY-SEVEN

A stunned silence fell.

Observe! Elodie thought.

Master Uwald's eyebrows were raised. He wagged his head from side to side as if he were considering a wager. But he seemed calm as ever, contrasted with Master Tuomo, whose face had mottled a dangerous red and white and whose eyes switched from the entry door to the windows high in the wall, too high to reach even standing on a table.

High Brunka Marya saw, too. "Master Tuomo, dear, if you're imagining breaking out, you won't succeed. You know how a rainbow tingles and stings. You won't be able to go through, not even if you ram the door with something. The pain will be too great."

"My sons!"

"You'll get news of them. If the Replica isn't found, they can visit you here."

Ludda-bee announced, "It's nothing to me." Followed by another bee, she marched back toward the kitchen, passing Johan-bee, who was rocking more rapidly than usual. She jogged his elbow. "You look like a sea horse, you booby." She disappeared into the kitchen.

A red-faced Johan-bee changed to shifting from side to side, foot to foot.

Albin whispered to Elodie, "The Replica will be found. Don't worry."

But she couldn't help it. They both knew her parents' Potluck Farm depended almost as much on him as on her father. If he were held here, the farm would fail.

He pressed a roll into her hand. "I saved this for you from breakfast."

How thoughtful he was. She took a bite.

Dror-bee said, "You mean I won't be allowed to help farmers in the spring?"

"I hope we'll find the thief long before then, but otherwise, you will not."

His voice rising, he added, "But that's the joy in being a bee, the only joy. That's what I delight in."

"I know, pup."

Mistress Sirka, always hovering, put an arm around his shoulder, and for once he let her, even leaned into her.

After another minute, bees and guests returned to their appointed tasks, except for Master Uwald, who lingered. He folded his arms and said nothing.

Elodie stayed to see what would happen. Master Robbie stayed, too.

The high brunka smiled. "Am I to be afraid, Master Uwald?"

"You may be whatever you like."

Elodie hadn't seen him angry before. His fury was cold, the frost evident in a whiteness around his nostrils and in the pinched lines between his eyebrows.

"I am Master Robbie's guardian. I cannot care for him if he leaves and I stay."

"You'd like to imprison him?"

"I will not be offered an impossible choice, a bet I cannot win."

High Brunka Marya seemed to soften. "I'm sorry, dear."

How strange for Master Robbie to be so loved by a man who was almost a stranger.

Master Robbie clenched the hand holding his cloak closed. He felt her eyes and shook his head at her. Poor Master Uwald, she thought, unloved again.

"Then you'll let us go," Master Uwald said.

"No."

"You can't think I'm the thief."

"I can't let you go and keep the others."

"You can. I'm *Master Uwald of Nockess Farm*, Marya. They'll understand."

Elodie thought they probably would. The owner of Nockess Farm was above everyone else.

He went on. "I'll make sure Tuomo's sons are safe and come back here."

"You're staying, Master Uwald, dear."

The chill fairly glittered. "The earl will be told you're holding me. You'll regret this."

"I'll never regret anything as much as letting the Replica be stolen."

Master Uwald stalked away, but he stopped to pat Master Robbie's shoulder. "Don't fret. This isn't the end."

Deeter-bee shuffled to the high brunka. While Elodie watched his slow approach, she decided IT would approve the high brunka's measure. She imagined IT saying, High Brunka Marya is roiling the murky depths of this theft and may force the thief to the surface.

Deeter-bee arrived. "Marya, if you keep this up, you'll interrupt history. Events won't progress as they're meant to."

"I won't let the villains leave."

"If you let them go, they'll be more likely to reveal themselves. You may catch them recovering the Replica or selling it."

"They may evade us for years. I don't want them to have a minute of enjoyment."

Elodie wondered if Deeter-bee could be the thief—just to make history.

He left the high brunka and made his slow way back to his bench.

Elodie stepped closer to the high brunka.

"You, too, lamb?"

"Is someone taking care of Nesspa and the other beasts?"

Her shoulders relaxed. "Certainly. The bees who searched the stable are caring for them. They're also searching the area outside. They've all been here more than seven years, the most trustworthy, as Masteress Meenore recommended. The Oase has a cottage not far from the stable, which is where they're sleeping at night."

Satisfied, Elodie stepped back with Master Robbie to see who else might come forward, but no one did. Feeling bold, she took his hand and tugged him to the southwest corner of the great hall, where they'd be farthest from anyone, although the high brunka would be able to hear them.

"What have we learned?" She shivered and wished for her masteress. "We have to deduce and in—"

"And not be reckless," he said, teasing her.

She shrugged. "That, too."

"Why was Master Uwald—er, *Grand*—so angry now when he wasn't before? Let's deduce that."

Elodie thought the answer obvious. "He doesn't want to lose you."

His nose turned pink again. "He knows me as little as I know him."

Master Robbie probably reminded Master Uwald of his first love. He might imagine he did know his ward. And—this was less admirable—Master Robbie might represent a wager Master Uwald had won in the end, a wager with himself or with his fate.

Master Robbie had his own explanation. "Maybe he thought he could go home after Zertrum explodes. He still owns his land, and he trusts his luck. High Brunka Marya is taking his luck away from him."

That was possible.

"Good fortune for Mistress Sirka," Master Robbie said. "She may have years to spend with Dror-bee."

The two were at the north-wall fireplace, talking. Or Mistress Sirka was talking and Dror-bee was nodding ardently.

Elodie said, "Could she have taken the Replica to make the high brunka imprison them?"

This seemed unlikely to both of them. Master Robbie said, "She couldn't guess what High Brunka Marya would do."

Albin, who had been deducing on his own, joined them. "Lady El, the lowly helper, foresees . . ." He abandoned the role of narrator. "Someone is likely to act rashly, perhaps violently, to get out of this jail. It may be the thief or anyone. Keep your distance from them all."

"In danger from me?" Master Robbie sounded almost as outraged as Master Tuomo.

"From everyone."

"Not from Master Robbie," Elodie hastened to say. "My masteress trusts him. And I can't keep my distance. IT asked us to investigate together."

"Then I'll remain with you both. Lady El, sit with me at meals."

She nodded. She could do that much.

If harm came to her, Masteress Meenore would certainly find the thief and would show ITs rage in heat and fire. This idea gave little comfort.

CHAPTER THIRTY-EIGHT

n early afternoon, His Lordship-as-a-horse swam the icy Fluce River with Widow Fridda and her daughters on his back. The donkey stood on the bank, brayed once, and plunged in, too.

On the other side, they climbed, crossed the road from Zee, and climbed again. After half an hour, a quarter mile above the Fluce, the horse knelt so his charges could dismount on a ledge in front of the caves of Svye Mountain. As they did so, the donkey arrived and began to munch snow a yard from where Goodman Otto and another man stood looking down over the river.

"How lucky you found a horse," Goodman Otto said. "That ogre didn't help after all. I'm not surprised."

The oldest girl began, "He—"

"Hush!" The widow handed her baby to the girl and

unloaded the pile of His Lordship's clothes from the horse's back. "Girls, close your eyes."

The horse vibrated. After a minute, Count Jonty Um donned his homespun tunic, cloak, and boots. Goodman Otto had the grace to blush.

The twins and the three-year-old hurried to him and hugged his legs.

The older girl smiled shyly. "He saved us."

Fee fi! His Lordship thought of becoming the monkey for happiness.

"I'm sure we're grateful, Your Countship." Goodman Otto touched the hood of his cloak in a gesture of respect.

"Grateful!" Widow Fridda picked up her satchels. "Grateful is a pebble. We owe him a boulder, a mountain all to himself." Her grim face softened; her lip trembled; her eyes were wet. "Arnulf's bees are nothing to him for aid."

The bolder twin added, "There never was a nicer horse."

"Are any bees in the nearest cave?" His Lordship tilted his head at it. The opening draped too low for him to enter without crawling.

"They went back to help others."

The man who hadn't spoken blurted out, "My brother! Sir . . . I couldn't bring him. He's mad and fought me off. The bees won't be able to handle him. He'll die unless you can get him."

"Where is he?"

"It's not far, not even a quarter way up the mountain." The man gave him detailed instructions. "You'll know him. He's raving."

His Lordship didn't hesitate. Too late now, with the mountain so close to exploding, to fly to the Oase. Meenore, he thought, it's all up to you.

"Wait!" The widow rummaged in one of her sacks. "Here." She held a loaf of bread out to him. "Take care!"

His Lordship took the loaf and smiled his sweet smile, which caused the widow to blush. He began the descent to the river, devouring the bread as he went. On the riverbank, he stripped and waded in, holding his clothing over his head. Fee fi! The water was cold.

CHAPTER THIRTY-NINE

asteress Meenore found Brunka Arnulf helping an aged couple into a sledge harnessed to an underfed donkey. Zertrum rumbled steadily beneath ITs claws.

The old people cried out in terror at the sight of IT, and the frightened donkey strained against its traces, beginning its slow progress downhill, the skis of the sledge scraping, bumping, and only occasionally gliding.

Brunka Arnulf pushed through the snow to IT. When he came close, he put his hand over his nose.

ITs smoke blued, an embarrassed dragon. "You are unsurprised and not much afraid at the sight of me."

"It's a time of marvels. A kindly ogre and now you."

"What do you know of His Lordship's whereabouts?"

"You are called Masteress . . .?"

"Mccnore. What took place during his visit?"

"I answered his questions, and he flew away. Oh, and I gave him food."

"Have you seen him since?"

"I repeat: He flew away."

IT scratched ITs earhole. "You evaded my question, and thus I deduce you *have* seen him since."

But the brunka wouldn't admit to lying. ITs worry mounted that some ill had befallen His Lordship.

"Tell me what you told him."

Brunka Arnulf ticked the items off on his fingers. "Dror may be angry at his family for sending him away. He's gone to be a bee at the Oase. The barber-surgeon Mistress Sirka left, too. I was told that he and she were to be wed, but I don't know the truth of that."

IT wondered if Dror-bee had been feigning indifference toward her.

"No one here is angry at me or brunkas in general or bees or Zertrum itself. Master Uwald and Master Tuomo and his sons are off the mountain."

"His sons, too? You are certain of this as unassailable fact?"

"I am."

Master Tuomo lied about his sons? "You have told me who the thief is, which His Lordship would have done long ago if he had returned to me. If you delayed him or

217

caused harm to come to him and the mountain spews, the destruction will be on your head."

Brunka Arnulf raised his eyebrows.

"Yes, on your head." ITs smoke turned rosy. "On the thief's head first and yours second, and, should you survive, a dragon's wrath will be on your entire person, not merely your head." IT rose in the air and flew south.

Tuomo, IT thought, you can give Elodie mansioning lessons. The smoke trailing behind IT glowed crimson. Did you have an ally? Who?

IT soared on, belching fire.

CHAPTER FORTY

he noon meal had not appeared, but now, midafternoon, Ludda-bee brought a loaded tray out from the kitchen, followed by a bee ringing a bell.

No one moved toward the table.

Clatter! Ludda-bee set down her tray, wrested the bell from her companion, and rang it furiously. "I did not cook for people to fast."

Six pairs of bees entered through both of the interior doors, coming from their searches of the many chambers of the Oase. Soon everyone was seated. Ludda-bee took the stool at the bottom of the table, facing—a long way away—the high brunka, each of them half a table length from Elodie, who sat between Albin and Master Robbie.

The rainbow colors on the entry door had not

diminished. Elodie wondered if her masteress or His Lordship were hungry and imagining a meal such as this, another feast: beets again, these pickled; pottage; bread; a wheel of cheese, of course; hard-boiled eggs rolled in oil and chopped rosemary; dried meats; and a savory bread pudding.

She ignored the lump in her throat and smiled at Albin. "What do you think of Masteress Meenore?"

"I think the heroine had an adventure in Two Castles, and *her* masteress was part of it." He helped her to the pudding. "Home will be dull after that. I wonder if she'll be sorry when we get there."

"Sorry? I can't wait." She whispered in his ear, "But I won't stay." Then, in an ordinary voice: "I even miss the geese."

He squeezed her shoulder. They both knew she hated herding. He'd told her she wasn't meant for a quiet life.

Master Robbie shared a chunk of dried roast boar from his bowl with her. In return she passed him a heaping spoonful of beets.

She wished the table were round so she could view everyone. As it was, she couldn't see most of those on the side with her. She had a partial view of Master Uwald only because Master Robbie didn't entirely block him, and she saw that his face was still locked in anger.

Johan-bee, who had been replaced as a door guard,

and Dror-bee, with Mistress Sirka faithfully at his side, sat across from Elodie. As she watched, Mistress Sirka served Dror-bee pottage and slipped in the bolus, the herbal love pill that Master Robbie had seen. Or this one could be made of other herbs, poisonous ones. She did it cleverly, holding the palm of her hand level with the lip of the bowl. High Brunka Marya, staring into space above everyone's head, didn't see. Only Johan-bee's eyes and Elodie's were on Mistress Sirka's hand.

He said nothing.

Should she let it go, too, and see what happened, in case it might be connected with the theft of the Replica?

No! She couldn't let him be poisoned. What to do?

Dror-bee lifted his spoon.

"Dror-bee?"

The spoon hovered above his bowl. "Yes?"

What to say? "Er . . . does your father's farm grow cabbages?"

"Yes." The spoon didn't move, but it wouldn't stay still forever.

"What's the biggest one he ever grew?" Farmers competed.

He put down the spoon and smiled and made a circle of his arms out across Mistress Sirka's face and the face of the bee next to him. "It weighed more than you."

Master Robbie stared at Elodie. Albin grinned, certainly

knowing she was mansioning.

But what to do? Mmm.

He picked up his spoon.

She picked up an egg. Let this work! It didn't have far to travel.

He dipped his spoon into the bowl.

She squeezed the oiled egg, which flew out of her hand, across the table, and landed in his pottage, splashing broth, herbs, beans, and shreds of meat.

CHAPTER FORTY-ONE

ount Jonty Um was able to go faster as himself than as a horse. His ogre brain could make quicker judgments about where to step; his long legs fairly ate up the ground, the ankle-deep snow hardly an obstacle. He had to stop only once, when the ground shook and stones popped through the snow. But the paroxysm lasted only a few seconds. The earth settled, and he was off again, his heart drumming in his ears.

In less than an hour he found the stand of evergreens, the cottage with the blue stool next to the door, and the lunatic pacing and shouting outside. Fee fi! When the man saw His Lordship, he cowered and gibbered softly.

Pity won against the count's anger at being feared. He hurried to the stand of trees and waited until the ranting began again, which he hoped meant he'd been forgotten.

Before shape-shifting, he wished he'd left his clothes with Widow Fridda. There was nothing for it, however. Telling himself over and over what he had to do, hoping the strategy would succeed, he shifted.

A minute later a monkey, smiling an enormous merry smile, stepped out from behind the trees. The man laughed to see him, a happy, ordinary laugh. The monkey held out his hand. The man took it and exchanged his shouts for coos and soft babbling. They started down the mountain, the monkey comically raising his feet out of the snow with every step.

CHAPTER FORTY-TWO

asteress Meenore flew laboriously above the southern slope of Zertrum. Without sleep last night and with little sleep the night before, IT feared nodding off and falling out of the sky.

Below lay farmland such as IT hadn't seen before on Lahnt, which seemed impoverished everywhere else: neat fields fenced into squares, orchards, and a house, a large structure of stone and wood, surrounded by barns, sheds, and several wattle-and-daub cottages. A drift of pigs, dozens of them, wandered among the buildings, rooting through the snow. This must be Master Uwald's Nockess Farm.

Curious, IT circled high enough not to be heard. At this height and with the sun near the horizon, ITs shadow became near invisible.

Supervised by a plump man with a pronounced limp, laborers brought goods out of the house and loaded two sledges that were hitched to oxen. What idiocy! The people should have been saving themselves. The limping man should already have ridden an ox or a horse out of danger.

Who was he, to be giving orders when the master and his steward were away?

On the mountain above the house, a dozen shepherds were driving flocks of geese, sheep, and goats slowly through the snow. More fools.

IT heard a deep groan. The entire slope undulated, then returned to solidity, but altered. A cottage collapsed. The pigs galloped here and there, squealing. A jagged crack divided the field that the herders had been crossing. Several sheep disappeared into the crack. The beasts ran in all directions. A goatherd lay trapped, his legs hidden beneath a boulder.

Zertrum's peak glowed red as if it were the mouth of a fellow dragon.

IT stopped circling and flew south toward the Oase and Elodie and the villain Tuomo.

But the trapped man plagued IT. The other herders wouldn't be able to lift the boulder. To dig him out would take time, if they'd stay to do it, and, meanwhile, there might be more tremors.

IT thought, I am no fairy god-dragon. The idiot herder should have fled at the first sign of the volcano. Elodie needs me.

But IT would blame ITself if the man died. IT turned and beat ITs way back to the mountain.

CHAPTER FORTY-THREE

"Oh my! I'm sorry! My hands were greasy." Elodie stood. "Let me get you a clean bowl."

Ludda-bee jumped up, too. "Look! A fellow oaf, Johan. Sit, girl. I'll clean up." She hurried into the kitchen, trailed by another bee.

Elodie sat.

"The girl isn't awkward." Mistress Sirka smiled her blazing, untamed smile at Elodie. "She contrived it. I was putting a love potion in your pottage, Dror, love."

"What?" Dror-bee looked confused. "You did?"

"You want a sign." She touched his cheek softly with the back of her hand. "It's a sign I love you."

Elodie looked away, turned back again, didn't know where to fix her eyes.

Master Uwald said dryly, "We'd all have had the sign

when he shared from his bowl."

"I'd have liked to try it," Master Robbie said.

Smiles around the table.

Albin whispered, "Lady El, you've made a conquest."

She blushed.

Master Uwald said, "A love potion is dangerous, son, and who knows what was really in it."

Sounding actually genial, Master Tuomo said, "I think you don't need it, boy."

Master Robbie blushed.

His big eyes shining, Dror-bee smiled at Mistress Sirka. "Do you think you might love me again?" she asked.

"Again?" Master Tuomo roared. "He loved you before? You took the Replica! The two of you, to punish the family that spurned him. Where is it?"

Angry and prosperous, Elodie thought, unconvinced that Mistress Sirka was the thief.

"I would have taken it." Mistress Sirka leaned across the table toward Master Tuomo. "Hair and teeth! If he wanted revenge, I would have taken the Replica if I could."

"But I've had my sign." Dror-bee turned to the high brunka. "Marya, I'm finished being a bee, now that I know a brunka can stop me from doing what pleases me: helping farmers."

Mistress Sirka's face was suffused with happiness.

Ludda-bee returned with a clean bowl and a cloth,

which she spread over the stained patch of tablecloth.

"High Brunka," Master Tuomo said, "what do you think of Sirka as the thief?"

"Dear Master Tuomo . . ." The high brunka sounded weary. "One or two of you took it, which includes you, Mistress Sirka, sweet. But I haven't singled you out. However, I'm willing to entertain accusations."

To Elodie's surprise, Dror-bee—Goodman Dror now—spoke. "I have one, but he's just a boy."

Elodie felt Master Robbie straighten next to her.

Goodman Dror continued. "I doubt he did it. You must know, Marya. You, too, Deeter and Master Uwald."

Master Uwald snapped, "That has nothing to do with this."

"What, er, Grand?"

"Nothing. Never mind."

"What, High Brunka?"

Her face was regretful. "Pup, your grandfather was the original thief."

Lambs and calves!

"He was?"

Did he really not know? Elodie wondered.

Deeter-bee said, "History rarely circles back so neatly."

"Why didn't Grandmother tell me?"

"He's too young to steal anything." Ursa-bee glared at Goodman Dror.

"I didn't say he did it!"

"Of course he didn't." Master Uwald stood, then sat. "The subject is closed. Robbie, eat your pottage."

Master Robbie whispered urgently to Elodie, "I'm not a thief."

What if he is? she thought.

She could barely credit it, and she wondered if Goodman Dror had told about the grandfather just to make everyone forget Master Tuomo's accusation.

Still, what if Master Robbie had placed the handkerchief that weeps in the Turtle Room? He might have known about it and stolen it before the high brunka showed it to him and Master Uwald. The Oase's relics weren't a secret. Or his accomplice might have taken the handkerchief before they became partners. Master Robbie would be an excellent choice as the one to place it and start it weeping—agile, quick, light on his feet.

But why?

With the money from the Replica, he wouldn't have to live with Master Uwald.

Ludda-bee said, "Johan, you are an ugly sight, chewing with that tooth medicine bumping up and down in your cheek. You should take it out at mealtimes."

He did nothing! Elodie thought indignantly.

Johan-bee's face reddened alarmingly. "No matter what, you make fun of me. A mountain may explode, but you still mock me." He reached for the wheel of cheese and threw it at Ludda-bee, who raised her arm just in time.

High Brunka Marya cried, "Johan, no one means—"

"Hold your tongue, Marya!"

Elodie gasped.

He continued, "You never helped me."

"I want you to help yourself."

"And now I am." He heaved the tureen of pottage across the table.

Luckily, the pottage had cooled. Elodie's cloak was spattered. Oatmeal and beans pocked Master Robbie's face, cap, and shoulders. The tureen itself hit Master Uwald in the shoulder.

Everyone but High Brunka Marya jumped up and backed away. Even Deeter-bee moved swiftly. Johan picked up the long bench, too long for him to control, and swung it wildly. People dived under the table or ducked. Elodie grabbed Master Robbie's hand as Albin pulled her out of range.

Calmly but loudly, the high brunka said, "Stop this, Jo—"

The bench continued its wild sweep and cracked her on the head. She fell.

CHAPTER FORTY-FOUR

Four herders surrounded the trapped man. One tipped a flask into his mouth so he might drink. Masteress Meenore flew lower, and all looked up, their mouths O's of astonishment. Surprise gave way to speed. Except for the trapped fellow, they fled, although the snow hindered them. They stumbled or fell entirely but were up again instantly, propelled by fear.

IT landed and tried to ignore the growling mountain.

The trapped herder shouted wordlessly, then coughed as ITs scent reached him. He choked out, "Don't . . . eat . . . me!"

ITs smoke went from blue to red, shame to anger. "That is what you fear at this juncture? You are hoping for one sort of death over another?" IT lumbered to the boulder and tried to lift it, but the boulder—squarish, taller than a man, shot through with orange veins—weighed too much.

"You're saving me?" The man let out a moan of pain.

Panting, IT puffed out, "First I must slice off slabs to lighten your captor. You will have time to enjoy my perfume." *Enh enh enh.*

The task would take an hour or more. ITs tail twitched impatiently.

"I am about to flame at the boulder, not at you."

Deep in ITs chest, ITs fire bellows expanded and contracted. A thick jet of white shot across a corner of the boulder.

Fire and smoke! This rock was dense. IT swallowed ITs flame to look. The line etched into the stone penetrated only about half a foot.

"We will be together for a while, Goodman . . ."

"Hame." His voice sounded strained. The pain must have been intense.

"And I am Masteress Meenore."

"Thank you for helping me." Another moan.

Helping you at the expense of time I cannot spare. While IT flamed again, IT used ITs common sense. Goodman Hame's information about Master Tuomo and his sons would be firsthand, unlike Brunka Arnulf's.

When IT stopped flaming, the gash had more than doubled in depth.

"I must rest a moment." A lie. Flaming didn't tire IT. "We may indulge in conversation. This is Nockess Farm, is it not?"

Goodman Hame nodded.

"Brunka Arnulf informed me that Master Tuomo's sons are gone from the estate. Is that so?"

He nodded again.

"I suppose Master Tuomo sent them on some errand."

He shook his head.

Mmm. "No? Then why did they leave?"

Goodman Hame spoke with difficulty. "Master Uwald sent them to his cousin's wedding because he had to travel to Zee and couldn't go."

"Do you know if Master Tuomo was present when the order was given?"

"Only Master Uwald."

IT flamed again, ITs mind as afire as ITs snout. Uwald?

"He told us . . ." Goodman Hame forced the words out. "All of us herders and servants . . ."

"Yes?"

". . . to take a holiday while he was away." He paused for breath. "But Master Tuomo *was* there then, and he said the farm couldn't spare us. . . ." Another pause. "He may have killed me. . . . Curse him!"

Curses on the wrong man. It *was* Uwald! But why

destroy his own land? "You are not yet a corpse."

"And now . . . someone has come who says he's our new master."

Master Uwald sold his farm? And then decided to destroy it? No . . . Oho! Not sold. Master Uwald had lost Nockess Farm in a wager. His luck had failed him.

IT flamed again and sliced through the remaining stone. The chunk fell away, but the boulder remained too heavy.

"Goodman Hame, is the man with the limp the new owner?"

He nodded.

IT considered flying off and leaving Goodman Hame to the mountain's mercy. Better to reach the Oase and Uwald in time. But despite the reasonableness of sacrificing one to save many, IT found that IT couldn't leave the man.

Had affection for Elodie softened ITs resolve and soaked ITs heart in sentiment?

IT flamed again at the boulder. Master Uwald, old and frail as he was, couldn't have acted alone. Two thieves, without a doubt. Who was his accomplice?

When IT stopped to view ITs progress, Goodman Hame interrupted ITs thoughts.

"Beg pardon . . . Are you a boy dragon or a girl dragon? Boy, right?"

How quickly terror fades, IT thought regretfully. IT flamed again. If Master Uwald stole the Replica he'd still be rich, but the winner would own the land after the mountain cooled. However, if the winner were on Zertrum when the volcano spewed, he would very likely perish. So Master Uwald must have promised to cede the property on a certain date.

Of course, the man might ride his horse off the mountain at the first tremor. However, Master Uwald knew the winner's character and predicted he'd stay on his new property as long as he believed he might, which would really be too long, and the evidence of the bet, presumably in the winner's possession, would be incinerated with him.

IT couldn't be sure if the fateful bet had occurred before or after Master Uwald knew Master Robbie would be his ward, but IT suspected that the game took place after.

Master Uwald's plan had been clever, even diabolical.

IT swore that in one respect, at least, the plot would fail.

CHAPTER FORTY-FIVE

eople rushed to High Brunka Marya. Elodie would have, too, but Albin held her in place. Master Uwald, who had a similar grip on Master Robbie, remained with them.

Elodie wondered what her masteress would expect her to do.

Think, Lodie!

She didn't know what to think.

Observe, Lodie!

That she could do.

The pairs of bees who guarded the interior exits had left their posts.

Lambs and calves! The rainbow colors over the entry door were gone. Was the high brunka dead?

No one else seemed to have noticed the door.

Mistress Sirka cried, "She's breathing!"

Elodie broke free of Albin and pushed into the crowd.

Mistress Sirka sat on the floor. Gently, she lifted High Brunka Marya's shoulders and head into her lap. "Someone, get my sack. Hurry!" She touched the violet bump that was rising on High Brunka Marya's forehead.

Two bees hurried out of the hall. The high brunka's mouth hung open. Her skin had a yellow cast, unlike its usual ruddy tone. Contrasted with her slack jaw, her eyes were squeezed shut. Her fingertips looked ordinary, without any sign of rainbows.

"Can I help?" Ursa-bee hovered behind Mistress Sirka's shoulder.

Standing near the high brunka's knees, Johan-bee rocked back and forth. He bit his knuckles, his eyes wide and confused.

Ludda-bee, next to him, slapped him across the face, reaching high to do so. Then, sobbing into her apron, she broke out of the crowd. Johan-bee seemed not to notice the slap or her departure.

Elodie discovered herself surrounded by Albin, Master Robbie, and Master Uwald, who had shoved their way in, too.

Master Tuomo, on the other side of the fallen high brunka, said, "They pushed him too far. These are circumstances that snap a man's control."

Master Uwald patted Master Robbie's shoulder, then sidled to Johan-bee and led him away. Elodie twisted out of the crowd to see where they went, which was to the south fireplace. Master Uwald spoke to him there, while Johan-bee continued to rock, his hands over his face. How kind Master Uwald was to take pity on him, when half his own cloak was soaked with broth and, if the tureen had hit him a little higher, he might have been as injured as the high brunka.

After a minute or two, Master Tuomo started across the great hall toward the two of them.

Why? Elodie thought. If only she had a brunka's hearing. And now the high brunka didn't have it either. The thieves, if there were two after all, could plot without being overheard.

And they could leave.

Elodie returned to the middle of the knot of people.

Mistress Sirka murmured, "I've never dosed a brunka before."

Elodie wondered if the high brunka's mind was alert. She said firmly, "I'm so glad we found"—louder—"the Replica."

High Brunka Marya didn't stir. Everyone else looked at Elodie.

She shrugged. "I thought that might wake her."

Albin said, "An excellent notion, Lady El."

The bees returned with Mistress Sirka's satchel.

The barber-surgeon rummaged inside for a netted sack of little jars. She picked one, unstopped it, and spread an ointment over the lump on High Brunka Marya's forehead. She found another jar, which she opened and waved under the high brunka's nose.

"What will those do?" Ursa-bee asked.

"The one under her nose wakes people who've fainted. The salve brings down swelling in people and, I hope, brunkas." Mistress Sirka took off High Brunka Marya's cap to explore her skull with her fingers. "Two more bumps." She applied ointment to these bumps, too.

"Brunka skulls are thick," Deeter-bee said. "We have a book on the anatomy of the brunka. There's granite in their bones."

Good! Excellent!

But what if Mistress Sirka were really doing harm to the high brunka? Elodie thought. What if the barber-surgeon and Goodman Dror were the thieves, and the high brunka's injury would allow them to escape, as long as she didn't wake quickly?

Johan-bee and his companions returned.

He knelt by her, across from Ursa-bee. "I'm sorry, Marya. I didn't mean to hurt anyone."

Several bees busied themselves putting the great hall back in order. Two piled dishes on Ludda-bee's tray. A bee carried the cider pitcher into the kitchen, not bothering to leave paired with another bee.

"Look!" Master Tuomo cried. "The rainbow is gone."

Elodie thought, It's all falling apart.

Using the tablecloth, a bee mopped up the pottage on the floor, leaving a circle cleared of rushes.

Albin whispered to Elodie, "I'm taking you home, Lady El."

No!

CHAPTER FORTY-SIX

s a monkey, His Lordship delivered the madman to his brother and started back to Zertrum. He didn't shape-shift into himself until he crossed the river. The ground had become unsteady: softening, hardening, shifting. Distant human cries flared up and died down. He followed the nearest voice.

CHAPTER FORTY-SEVEN

won't go." Elodie took Albin's hand and tugged him toward the northwest corner of the great hall, the corner not far from the unguarded entrance. The windows high in the wall barely glistened. The day had almost ended.

When they reached the corner she—thoughtlessly—faced Albin with her back to the entrance. "We can't leave," she whispered. "Zertrum will explode if I don't find the—"

"You, Lady El? A mansioner? We enact the great events after they—"

"I'm a detecting dragon's assistant *and* a mansioner." She felt proud, declaring herself.

"Apologies, Lady El, but we must leave. Your parents would want you to, and I serve them."

Doubtless they would. There was no answer to that, but she couldn't go.

Albin went on with his argument. "Your safety means more to them—and to me—than the life of anyone on Zertrum."

"Listen . . ." An idea was coming. She felt its approach but couldn't grasp it. "Er . . . all the guests will leave . . . and if the thief—or thieves—is a bee, he or she will leave, too, with some excuse. The thief will go, if not tomorrow, then soon, because the Replica has to be sold or its worth doesn't matter. Right?"

"I suppose." Albin folded his arms.

"Er . . . but the brunkas and the other bees won't stop looking for him or her or them. Um . . . it won't matter to them that Zertrum has already spewed."

"We'll be safe at home, eating your mother's excellent pottage."

She'd be herding geese, and by then Masteress Meenore or His Lordship or both might have died in the volcano.

The idea arrived, although she hadn't expected it to be so frightening. "The thieves will want to be safe, too. Because of them, we'll still be in danger."

Albin wasn't used to deducing. "How do you come to that?"

"Because the thieves will plot to silence everyone who was here during the theft. Don't you see? There are clues even if we don't recognize them yet. One may be that Mistress Sirka tried to dose Dror-bee—I mean, Goodman Dror—with what she says was a love potion, or that Master Robbie's grandfather was the last thief, or that Ludda-bee hates everyone and everything except cooking. Or something else."

Albin's eyes were tight on her, concentrating as only a mansioner can.

"The innocent will go home. Some of us will try to forget, and some of us will try to remember. One morning, you or I or Master Robbie or another of us will sit up in bed with all the pieces fitted together." Her heart began to gallop. "The thief will dread that morning, and he or she—who will have killed many on Zertrum—will have the wealth to kill us, too, not in person, but by using hirelings. You may not come back from fixing a fence. I may not return from herding. Master Uwald may be poisoned. Master Robbie may seem to have run away. Mistress—"

"Enough. I understand."

"One more thing. If everyone stays here, that can't happen. We're safest here."

He thought about it. "Lady El, Lady El. All right. We stay. For now."

She took his hand and turned to go back to the others—and discovered her mistake. She had stopped observing.

The entrance, without the rainbow glow, remained

unguarded, and the great hall had half emptied.

Lambs and calves! Had the thieves escaped already? Escaped with the Replica?

Mistress Sirka continued to tend High Brunka Marya, who had been moved onto a pallet. Ursa-bee and Goodman Dror hovered nearby.

Several other bees, not in pairs, searched the shelves and cupboards. Deeter-bee watched from a bench by the fireplace outside the kitchen.

But Masters Robbie, Tuomo, and Uwald, as well as Johan-bee and Ludda-bee, were gone.

"Albin, did you see anyone leave the Oase?"

"My eyes were on you, Lady El."

She called out, "Has anybody gone out?"

Ursa-bee answered, "No one, little mistress."

Relief flooded her. "Oh, good. Thank you." Trailed by Albin, she went to the entrance, leaned against the heavy door, and felt the cold of a November evening penetrate her shoulders.

Albin smiled fondly at her and said a mansioner's proverb: "'A butterfly cannot portray a bear.' You can't be a guard, and I know only stage fighting."

"We have to stop whoever comes."

"Very well." He bowed his most elaborate bow. "I hope the farmer's helper doesn't have to die for the heroine."

From the door that led to the corridor, Johan-bee

entered the great hall carrying a longbow, with a quiver of arrows on his back. What's more, he'd strapped a sword around his waist. As awkward as ever, he strode stiffly toward the entrance.

Johan-bee was the thief?

Her masteress had never deduced or induced him as a villain.

Armed as he was, they'd have to let him go.

CHAPTER FORTY-EIGHT

he sun sank below the horizon. Zertrum blew out a gob of fiery molten rock, which lit the gray sky with a second sunset as it dropped back into the mouth of the volcano.

Masteress Meenore thought the boulder reduced enough. IT heaved, and the rock rolled off the herder. By the half-light of dusk, IT saw that Goodman Hame's right leg had merely been scraped, but his left ankle was covered with dried blood and swollen to thrice the size of the other.

"We will leave in a moment. First, what is the name of your new master?"

"Erick."

"Excellent. Can you kneel?"

He proved he could by kneeling.

IT lowered ITself and extended a wing. "Spread your

cloak across my back. . . . Good. Now climb on. . . . You may crawl. You will not hurt my wings, which are nearly indestructible as well as beautiful. When I fly, refrain from touching my scales, which will be burning hot."

The man was in place. IT flapped ITs wings and sprang into the air, aware instantly of the difference in weight between Goodman Hame and Elodie.

Three wing flaps took IT above Master Uwald's house, where the limping man was just taking his place on a loaded sledge behind a team of oxen.

Below the house was a small field edged with pine trees. IT spiraled down.

"I thought you were saving me," Master Hame cried.

"I am." IT landed carefully, not so near the oxen, IT hoped, that they would bolt.

Too close. The terrified beasts broke the sledge out of the snow and began careering down the mountain.

Swearing a dozen dragon oaths, IT flew above the sledge as it crossed a snowy pasture and started onto a long ledge that ended in a cliff. Master Erick's cry rose thin and sharp as he pulled uselessly back on the reins.

IT set ITs teeth. I will not be the cause of this man's death. I will not be Uwald's instrument.

The oxen hurtled on.

I will do what I have never before attempted. IT swooped lower, ITs claws extended.

The first ox plunged over the cliff.

Flapping ITs wings, acutely aware of Goodman Hame on ITs back, IT lifted portly Master Erick by his cloak and his tunic, deposited him in the snow, and landed at his side.

Master Erick waved his hand in front of his nose. "You almost killed me! And your smell may finish me off."

Zertrum's rumble rose in pitch and volume.

IT ignored the rudeness. "Master Uwald stole the Replica and hopes to contrive your death."

"No!" from Goodman Hame.

"He wouldn't dare!" from Master Erick.

"I hope to frustrate him. Goodman Hame here was trapped by a falling boulder and is injured. If you—"

"IT saved me, Master. You should—"

"Master Erick, do not delay. The mountain is not reliable. Spread your cloak over me. Sit on it. You will not be cold. Do not touch my scales when—"

The ledge they stood on trembled.

"Hurry!"

Master Erick scrambled up.

IT flapped ITs wings, but Master Erick was heavy! IT was still on the ground when the ledge collapsed beneath them.

CHAPTER FORTY-NINE

ohan-bee stopped at the stricken high brunka and rocked on his heels. His sword vibrated. "Is she better?"

Phew! Elodie thought. He isn't leaving. Then why the sword and longbow?

"No," Mistress Sirka said.

Goodman Dror, still standing at her side, chimed in. "She could die because of you, you clumsy clod."

Ursa-bee added, "Ludda meant no harm before. She can't help her sharp tongue."

Hoping to do some good, Elodie said, "I think it was unkind of her."

Johan-bee headed toward the door, where they were standing.

Oh no!

"Marya didn't want people to leave. Stand back." He had appointed himself armed door guard.

"We're not leaving," Albin said, making room for him. "Lady El persuaded me to stay."

"Step away. I don't want help. People call me useless, but I can do this, and I need little sleep."

What about when he wanted to use the garderobe?

Elodie and Albin moved a few feet to the side.

"Farther."

They obliged.

"That's a rare ability," Albin said encouragingly, "being able to stay awake. Do you really need the weapons? You can just shout and I'll help you. Someone else may get hurt."

"Only if they try to force their way through."

With Johan-bee's luck, he might stab himself—or his arrow might bounce off something, come back, and end his sad life. Or he might injure someone else, not meaning to, as he'd already hurt High Brunka Marya.

"Ursa-bee," Mistress Sirka said, "a drink of broth may do the high brunka good."

"I'll fetch it." She hurried to the kitchen.

"Where is everyone?" Elodie asked.

Johan-bee said, "Most of the bees are searching. Master Uwald and young Master Robbie are in their room, and Master Tuomo is in his."

Preparing to leave? Elodie thought.

"Ludda is cooking," Goodman Dror said. "She says the last meal was ruined."

Elodie had to hold herself back from laughing. While a brunka was insensible, while people and a precious ogre and dragon might be dying, while a mountain was on the point of exploding, a spiteful cook fussed over pottage and cabbage and beets. Why didn't she help with the search?

Because she was a thief and knew where the Replica was?

Just as Ursa-bee emerged from the kitchen with a mug of broth, the door to the corridor opened. Master Tuomo, carrying a satchel in each hand, marched in, followed by Master Uwald, similarly burdened. Master Robbie lagged behind, bearing a large velvet sack in one hand and a small burlap one in the other. His eyes sought Elodie.

"Only Master Uwald may leave." Johan-bee's right hand rested on the hilt of his sword; his left held his bow. His rocking slowed. "He's no thief."

No one could leave! Elodie thought. What to do?

Master Tuomo halted but didn't put his satchels down. His face reddened to scarlet.

"And Robbie." Master Uwald continued toward the door.

"Only you, Master Uwald."

Master Robbie stopped in the center of the great hall.

Master Uwald stopped, too, his face regretful. "I'll come back for you, son."

Elodie thought, Albin would never leave me behind. IT had, but IT was a dragon, and IT was hoping to save everyone.

What to do?

"If Marya awakens," Master Uwald added, "she'll let you come to me."

But the high brunka seemed far from waking. Mistress Sirka had to hold her mouth open to dribble in a thin stream of broth. "There you go. Isn't that good?"

"Johan-bee, what will he accomplish that I can't?" Master Tuomo's gruff voice was pleading. "He doesn't have sons on the mountain."

"Just Master Uwald."

"Because he was kind to you? I never teased you, did I?"

Johan-bee didn't answer.

The steward turned to his master. "What will you do when you leave, Uwald?"

"First I'll go to Brunka Keld and—"

"He'll be helping on Zertrum."

Keld was the brunka on Svye Mountain, just to the south of Zertrum.

"You're right."

Elodie felt one of ITs *Mmm*s bubble up. Master Uwald hadn't thought out what he'd do when he left here?

He went on. "I'll stop at the first cottage and tell them to go to Poldie."

Poldie was the brunka on Bisselberg, the mountain Elodie and her friends had passed on their way north.

"He'll come with bees who can search outside here and bring food. Then—"

"High Brunka Marya already has bees looking outside," Elodie broke in. "She said so. They're also taking care of the dog who came with us." You don't have to go for that reason, she thought.

Master Uwald said, "Oh?" and blinked. After a pause—for a moment too long—he added, "Excellent news."

Mmm.

But Master Uwald couldn't be the thief. He owned Nockess Farm on Zertrum.

"Not excellent news for the thieves." Mistress Sirka sounded amused.

What if the outside bees had found it, Elodie thought, and run off with it? Even bees might be tempted.

"Never mind," Master Uwald said. "Poldie will bring more bees to help inside and out. Tuomo, I'll go to Zertrum and see how bad it is at the farm. When I find your boys, I'll send them here."

"Just send one. As soon as the mountain dies down, the

others can get to work. But Johan-bee, I'm better suited to the task than Uwald."

"Only Master Uwald." Johan-bee stepped away from the door.

CHAPTER FIFTY

eating ITs wings frantically, IT managed to do what had to be done: keep ITs cargo on ITs back; not plummet; and gain altitude, although Master Erick felt as heavy as a boulder. When ITs flight steadied, IT flapped wearily south. Night had fallen—a charcoal, cloudy night. IT smelled more snow on the way.

Goodman Hame was silent except for an occasional groan, but Master Erick complained with every breath: The air was foul. ITs flight was uneven. He had a delicate stomach. His bottom was too hot, his head too cold.

IT was astonished he'd voice discontent to his bearer, who had only to tip a wing to drop him—which grew more tempting by the moment.

"Where are you taking us?" Master Erick demanded.

To the closest haven I can find in the dark, IT thought.

But IT saved ITs breath and didn't answer.

Master Erick said he'd always heard dragons were rude.

Goodman Hame said, "There are caves on Svye."

"Nearby?" IT asked.

"Yes. I've been there. Fly low, along the river."

CHAPTER FIFTY-ONE

is Lordship couldn't judge time here. After a half hour or an hour or ten minutes, the cries ahead became more distinct, a man's voice and a woman's, grunts and a few words: "Here." "Push." "I'm trying."

He saw a mound of stones with a few wooden posts protruding—a collapsed cottage. How could anyone be alive under there?

In a frenzy, His Lordship burrowed in, his hands like shovels, heaving rubble behind him.

Lower on the mountain, a gash—a chasm too broad for His Lordship to leap across—opened in the earth.

CHAPTER FIFTY-TWO

aster Uwald transferred both satchels to one hand and lifted a torch from a sconce beside the door.

"Wait!" Elodie cried.

Courteous as ever, he said, "What is it, young Mistress Elodie?"

"Er . . . travel is hazardous at night. Why not wait until morning?" When High Brunka Marya may have awakened and can stop you. "You won't get to Zertrum in time anyway."

"No, but I'll reach a cottager who can start for Bisselberg. Johan-bee, please."

Johan-bee pulled open the heavy door.

"Tuomo, watch over my boy. There's danger here. Don't let him be hurt."

"I won't."

Elodie sent Master Robbie an imploring look.

"Mast—um . . . Grand . . ."

"Yes?"

"I don't want you to leave me." Master Robbie, apparently a mansioner, too, twisted his mourning beads.

Master Uwald's smile melted. "Oh, my boy, my boy." He returned the torch to its holder, went to Master Robbie, and hugged him to his chest.

After a pause, Master Robbie's arms circled Master Uwald's waist.

Johan-bee stood awkwardly with the door open. The cold night air rolled in.

Ludda-bee entered from the kitchen, ringing her bell. After a minute she held the clapper to announce, "I made a light repast. I expect it to be eaten." She put her bell on the floor. "How is Marya?"

"The same." Mistress Sirka rubbed more ointment on her bumps.

"Too bad we don't have a real physician." Ludda-bee went to the corner where the tabletop and trestles were stowed. "Someone, help me."

It was best to do Ludda-bee's bidding. Goodman Dror, Ursa-bee, and the bees who were searching the great hall hurried to her. They began to assemble the table in its usual spot, not far from where the high brunka lay and near

Master Uwald and Master Robbie, who had just dropped their arms from their hug.

"Son . . ." Master Uwald coughed wetly, a tearful cough. "It's right that I go. Tuomo suffers from not knowing his sons' fate. Our laborers need me. Nockess Farm needs me."

"Master Uwald's the proper one to go." Ludda-bee set a trestle in place. "But he should eat something first. Johan, put down those weapons. You look ridiculous. You can help with the table if you don't trip over yourself."

Johan-bee smiled or bared his teeth, Elodie wasn't sure which. In one smooth movement, he nocked his longbow and aimed it at Ludda-bee.

Lambs and calves!

In a mock frightened voice Ludda-bee cried, "Oh, don't shoot me." She shook the trestle and made it rattle. "See how afraid I am."

He'll kill her! Elodie thought. "Don't do—"

Ursa-bee cried, "Johan, you—"

"Johan-bee," Master Uwald said silkily, "remember? We talked about this. Ludda-bee speaks harshly sometimes, but you rise—"

"I tell the truth!" Ludda-bee said. "Everyone needs to hear the truth."

Johan-bee lowered the bow.

"Now help me." Ludda-bee picked up one end of

another trestle. "Stop playing the fool."

"I'm guarding to keep people from leaving."

Ludda-bee opened her mouth for a rejoinder, which might have gotten her shot, but Master Robbie spoke first.

"Master Uwald"—he'd reverted to the term he found more congenial—"if you leave, I won't go with you when you return. High Brunka Marya told me I could live here."

Master Uwald shook his head as if unsure of what he'd heard. "Who . . . what?"

"If you stay now, I'll go with you later."

"Son, Marya wants to imprison me, all of us."

Ah. That's the crux of it, Elodie thought. He isn't a thief. He just can't bear losing his freedom.

The bees finished setting up the table and placing the benches. Deeter-bee lumbered to the end of a bench and sat. Ludda-bee stumped into the kitchen.

Elodie thought, I'm not nearly as brilliant as IT, but maybe the others would deduce along with me. "Er . . . Master Uwald . . ."

"Yes?"

"Everyone . . ." This would be the end of appearing dull witted, but she hadn't made much of a show of that anyway. "Masteress Meenore flew off in search of information, leaving me to continue unraveling the mystery, with Master Robbie's help."

He nodded. "Mistress Elodie is ITs assistant. IT *pays* her."

"The dragon thought you might help?" Master Uwald asked, sounding proud.

"IT said I have an 'original mind.'"

"I'll wager you do."

"They're children!" Master Tuomo cried.

In the voice of a mansioner narrator, Albin intoned, "'The foolishness of age, the wisdom of youth.'"

"Nonsense!"

Elodie went on as if Master Tuomo hadn't spoken. "IT may have been delayed." Injured or killed! "In the meanwhile, ITs method is to deduce and induce and—"

"Use common sense!"

Elodie nodded at Master Robbie. "Yes. But IT asks for others' opinions, too, especially when IT's thinking hard. IT liked Master Robbie's idea. That's why—"

"What idea, son?"

"That the thief might have made a replica of the Replica, and the actual Replica might have been stolen before High Brunka Marya showed it to us the first time."

"Ingenious!" Master Uwald clapped his hands.

"But then," Master Tuomo said, "Zertrum could have done its worst while we were still on it, or days ago."

Elodie didn't want Master Uwald to lose his enthusiasm. "Correct or not, it was clever. Masteress Meenore explained ITs thinking thus far to both of us. If we tell you, maybe all of us can determine what happened."

"Please stay, Grand."

Ludda-bee returned with a loaded tray. "I'm not laying out a full meal in the middle of the night." She put the tray down. "You'll have to make do with this."

No one moved.

Ludda-bee rang her bell and didn't stop ringing. People started toward the table. Elodie crouched to tie her bootlaces and delay sitting. Finally the clangor ceased. She stood and saw that almost everyone, including Master Uwald, was seated. Relief coursed through her. Only Johan-bee at the door and Mistress Sirka on the floor with the high brunka didn't join them. Johan-bee closed the door with a creak and a thud.

Ludda-bee occupied the stool at the head of the table, farthest into the room, closest to the high brunka. The other stool stood empty. Elodie, feeling presumptuous, took it. She wanted to be able to see everyone, and she could, excepting Johan-bee at his post behind her.

Albin sat at her right and a bee she hadn't met was at her left, until Master Robbie squirmed out of his place between Master Uwald and Ursa-bee and came around the table, where he squeezed onto the bench at her left.

Across from Master Uwald and Albin, Master Tuomo and Goodman Dror were on either side of Deeter-bee. The other places were filled by the bees who'd been searching the Oase beyond the great hall.

"I'll stay for the meal," Master Uwald said. "It would be foolish to leave hungry. Son, will that satisfy you?"

Master Robbie nodded.

Eat slowly, everyone! Elodie thought.

There seemed to be as many dishes as ever. No pottage, but a sausage-and-bean stew, along with poppy-seed rolls, spiced apples, long yellow beans, the eternal beets, and honey wafers.

Ludda-bee told Johan-bee to sit. When he told her twice and roared at her once that he wouldn't, she filled a bowl and brought it to him. He put down his bow to eat.

"Well, girl?" Master Tuomo demanded.

Elodie tried to quell the flutter in her stomach. "Deeter-bee, would you tell everyone where the Replica was hidden?"

He obliged and answered Master Tuomo's questions about who had known.

When the subject was exhausted, Elodie persuaded Ursa-bee to say what had happened when she'd been guarding and had heard the weeping.

As soon as she finished, Elodie asked Master Robbie to lay out ITs theory about what had happened. While he spoke, she worried about the next step, the deducing.

If only IT would blow the door open.

But she might get ITs help another way. Maybe she could *be* IT—shape-shift in a mansioner's fashion. Lambs and calves, could she?

Master Robbie ended with "Now we have to deduce and induce and use our common sense."

Elodie cleared her throat and glanced at Albin. Help me.

"Masters . . . Bees . . . Mistress . . . We'd certainly do better if my masteress were here, but if I mansion IT, IT may help us all think."

"Absurd!"

"Master Tuomo," Albin said, "if your sons survive, you can tell them and your grandchildren that you were fortunate enough to be present when Elodie of Lahnt mansioned."

Thank you, Albin!

"Oh, hush, Tuomo." Master Uwald smiled benevolently at her.

If you rush, you will bungle. In her own voice Elodie said, "If Masteress Meenore were really here, ITs smoke would rise in tight white circles, which mean dragon happiness. IT's always pleased to show off ITs unfathomable brilliance. Please imagine the smoke rings." She wished she could recline as IT would have, but she might lose everyone if she began moving benches.

She made her voice nasal. "When an object of great value is taken, there is never a lack, I mean, *dearth*"—she needed all the hard words she could command. Luckily, the mansioners' plays were a help—"of persons who would benefit from owning it. Let us consider you one by one."

CHAPTER FIFTY-THREE

he fires on Zertrum lit the north face of Svye.

Goodman Hame spotted the caves. "See? There!"

IT saw. A minute later, IT landed on the ledge, while everyone outside dashed inside.

Master Erick and Goodman Hame disembarked, the latter by crawling.

Goodman Hame shouted, "You can come out. IT's a good dragon."

Masteress Meenore's smoke reddened. Good at what? Good for what?

Lovers of the good ogre—everyone—poured out of the cave, eager to meet the good dragon, and began coughing.

"IT rescued us. IT lifted a boulder off me," Goodman

Hame announced. Then he fainted.

Several people surrounded him.

"And almost killed me." Master Erick couldn't keep the tidings to himself: "Uwald stole the Replica."

After an hour of Master Erick, IT thought, everyone will forgive Master Uwald. IT spied Brunka Arnulf and lumbered to the edge of the crowd, where the brunka joined IT.

"Did Master Uwald really steal the Replica?"

"Yes. Where is His Lordship?"

"Back on Zertrum, finding people and bringing them here."

"Is that why you lied to me before?"

"He'd been injured as a bird. He couldn't fly back to the Oase. But he's recovered, and I didn't want you to keep him from rescuing folks." Brunka Arnulf flicked out a short rainbow. "His heroism will live forever."

"I prefer he not begin his afterlife tonight. He owes me wages." IT stared across the river. In the chaos, His Lordship could be anywhere. Even a being twice his size might be impossible to find.

"The last time he delivered someone to the cave, I begged him to stay."

IT pondered.

Leave now and fly to Elodie?

Arrive at the Oase too late to save His Lordship but in time—possibly—to rescue her from Uwald and his accomplice?

Allow Nesspa to lose his master?

IT sneered at ITself for thinking of the well-being of a dog.

"Masteress?" Brunka Arnulf said.

"I am cogitating."

"His Lordship would search for you."

"He and I are not alike."

Although fire held no terror, IT could be buried if the mountain collapsed. A boulder could rip through one of ITs beautiful wings or shatter ITs skull and destroy ITs miraculous mind.

Moreover, if IT went after His Lordship, the folk of Lahnt would for all time dub IT a *good* dragon. That would gall.

"I have decided." IT pushed off the ledge and flapped back toward Zertrum.

Over the Fluce, unexpectedly—uselessly!—from the depths of ITs prodigious brain, surfaced the location of the Replica and the identity of the second thief. IT remembered the puppet's words: "Expectation misleads."

Think, Lodie!

But IT doubted that even her penetrating mind would derive the answer.

CHAPTER FIFTY-FOUR

lodie tapped a claw (fingernail) on the table. "Mistress Sirka and Goodman Dror have been proposed as the thieves by Master Tuomo, so let us consider them first."

"Again?" Mistress Sirka yawned.

"I beg your forgiveness, I mean, *indulgence*."

Master Robbie giggled.

Elodie wished he wouldn't. This wasn't a mere performance. "Master Tuomo exposed their motives: rage at Goodman Dror's family coupled with greed. The method—"

Ludda-bee burst out, "No one is eating! Eat!" She passed the plate of yellow beans in one direction, the beets in the other.

"The method the thieves used," Elodie continued as

people helped themselves and their neighbors to food, "we have already established. It will be the same whoever they are. The trouble, I mean, *difficulty*, is that neither knew where the Replica was hidden. Goodman Dror has not been a bee long enough to be told."

"Another bee may have told him," Master Tuomo said.

Elodie wished she knew the rest of the bees. She doubted the ones she knew would have told.

Deeter-bee came unexpectedly to her rescue. "Then we would have three thieves, or why else would the bee tell?"

Elodie made an O with her lips and blew a long stream of air. "Three is, er, an *unwieldy* number." What to say next? She wanted to deduce about Master Tuomo, but she was afraid of him. "Let us move along to another potential villain . . ." Who? ". . . Lodie's father's helper, her friend—"

"Hair and teeth!" Mistress Sirka cried. "Now open your eyes. Open—"

"What happened?" Johan-bee sounded more frightened than glad.

Elodie stepped away from the table to see the high brunka. Everyone else either stood or turned.

"Less than I hoped," Mistress Sirka said. "She moved her hand and a wee rainbow came out of her thumb. Then the hand dropped back and the rainbow faded."

"Is that good or bad?" Ursa-bee said.

"Could be either. She may be waking up or sinking deeper."

"Continue, Mistress Elodie," Master Uwald said. "I want to satisfy my son and set out."

Elodie thought, He wants to be off before he can be re-imprisoned.

Albin performed a seated bow. "You were about to accuse me, Lady— I mean, Masteress."

She sat again. "Indeed. Goodman Albin wanted passage money to rescue my assistant, who in fact needed no *succor*. Stealing the Replica to realize such a small sum may be likened to killing a flea with a cannon. Nonetheless, he was desperate. In a strange twist of fortune, he won more than enough dicing with Master Uwald, but that occurred after the theft, so—"

"I thought you never lose, Grand."

Albin spooned beets into Elodie's bowl. He said, "I believe that Master Uwald was kind enough to lose for my benefit."

Elodie saw Master Tuomo frown.

Deeter-bee put the frown into words. "Hard to lose on purpose at dicing. The game is pure luck."

"In truth, Goodman Albin ended my long good luck." Master Uwald helped himself to a second helping of spiced apples, his eyes on the serving bowl. "These are uncommonly good, Ludda-bee."

Elodie swallowed a spoonful of warm stew against the chill that ran through her. Master Uwald had just shown two signs of lying. She glanced at Albin and saw him looking at her. He'd noticed, too. Master Uwald hadn't met Master Robbie's eyes, and he'd said *In truth*. Her mansioner training had taught her that whatever followed that phrase was likely to be false. The game with Albin hadn't been the one that ended his luck. Master Uwald had lost before.

Did that matter?

It mattered if he'd lost Nockess Farm.

How could she accuse Master Uwald?

Albin did it for her. "Mansioners study people so we can play our roles truthfully. Begging your pardon—I think you lied about your loss to me being the first."

Master Uwald patted his lips with the tablecloth, leaving a lip-shaped, beet-colored stain. "How clever, to turn Mistress Elodie's accusation away from you."

Elodie nodded slowly, remembering ITs big head. "I will continue. Like Mistress Sirka and Goodman Dror, Goodman Albin came to the Oase with no knowledge of the whereabouts—"

"Uwald . . ." Master Tuomo's voice was quieter and more controlled than usual. He half stood to reach across the table and tap Master Uwald's left hand, which was on his bowl. "Did you lose Nockess in a wager?"

Master Uwald put down his spoon with care. "Certainly not." But he didn't meet Master Tuomo's eyes either.

"Masteress," Master Robbie said, "I'd like to deduce."

"Proceed." Would he help his guardian who loved him? Or would he prove what Elodie now felt certain to be true, that Master Uwald was one of the thieves?

"Yes, son?"

"Master Uwald told me he'd never lost a bet since Grandmother refused him. 'Lucky in gaming, unlucky not to have her,' he said. Another time, he said he had her now in me. I deduce he isn't lucky at gaming any—"

Master Uwald talked over Master Robbie. "I won every wager against your masteress, Mistress Elodie, didn't I?"

"My sons!" Master Tuomo reached across the table and pulled Master Uwald up by his shoulders. "If you killed them—"

"Tuomo!" Master Uwald cried.

Deeter-bee and another bee pulled Master Tuomo back, although he struggled against them.

Master Uwald whispered, "Your sons are fine."

"Say again?"

Master Uwald sat slowly with both hands on the table to lower himself. "I sent them to Ilse's wedding and told them not to tell you. I would never hurt your sons. Robbie, I'm not so bad as that."

It was an admission. Master Uwald was the thief.

He went on, "I tried to give the servants and herders a holiday, too, but you—"

"When did you lose Nockess? Where?"

"The night after the message came that Lilli died. I rode out to clear my mind and met travelers on the—"

"I gave my life to your land." Master Tuomo had switched from one grievance to another.

Who was Master Uwald's accomplice?

And where was the Replica?

High Brunka Marya groaned. In a weak voice she said, "Johan? Did you hit me?"

CHAPTER FIFTY-FIVE

asteress Meenore landed in a barren field about a quarter mile above a chasm. Plumes of smoke rose from fires that dotted the slopes.

IT surveyed ITs near surroundings. In this field, the snow remained in patches, but most had melted, leaving a meadow where only stones grew.

Earlier, IT had flown up the mountain almost to the terrifying peak, which belched flames but little molten rock—so far. From the heights, IT had descended gradually, to and fro, back and forth. Often, no matter how low IT glided, enough smoke smothered the ground to conceal a mob of ogres. IT had ignored the human cries that assailed ITs ears. If IT stopped for everyone in need, IT would never save His Lordship.

Count Jonty Um wouldn't be looking for anyone or calling out. Perhaps IT could call him. IT trumpeted,

> *"There was a dragon called Bertram*
> *who flew a long, long way to Zertrum*
> *then tumbled in a deep abyss*
> *and landed with a hoot and a hiss,*
> *that foolish, silly, idiot, heedless, nincompoop dragon*
> *called Bertram!"*

IT hardly heard ITself over the fire crackle and the crash of tumbling rocks, but, unable to devise a better plan, IT sang again, knowing, as it bellowed and bellowed, that nincompoop Bertram was really Meenore.

CHAPTER FIFTY-SIX

ohan-bee rocked rapidly heel-to-toe and stared fixedly straight ahead. "Yes, I hit you. I didn't mean to."

Master Uwald held out his arms. "Son . . ."

Master Robbie shook his head violently.

Mistress Sirka helped High Brunka Marya stand up.

"Slowly, please, dear." She leaned against the barber-surgeon. "I'm dizzy." Small rainbows flowed from her fingers. She shook her hands and the rainbows subsided.

Ludda-bee jumped off the high brunka's stool. "Here." She began to ladle everything into a bowl.

Master Uwald crooned softly in a longing tone, "Son . . . Son . . . . Son . . ."

Master Robbie looked just as he had when Elodie first

saw him: pink-tipped nose, red-rimmed eyes, hands on his mourning beads.

"Keep the stool, Ludda," High Brunka Marya said. "I'll just fall off. The bench will be better. And I can't eat yet."

Everyone shifted, and Mistress Sirka eased the high brunka onto the bench next to Goodman Dror, at the end farthest from the door and Johan-bee, who remained at his post. High Brunka Marya seemed to have forgotten about sealing the door with her rainbow.

Mistress Sirka sat at the very end, so that the high brunka was wedged between her and Goodman Dror. The barber-surgeon smiled triumphantly around the table. "I healed a brunka!"

"Johan," High Brunka Marya said, "I am disappointed in you. You behaved like an unruly ram, no matter how provoked you were. And now, why the longbow and sword?"

"To keep anyone from leaving."

"I see. Very well. Soon my rainbow will be able to do that again." She turned from one bee to another until she'd met the eyes of every one. "No one is to tease Johan anymore. I forbid it. He committed an error, but he deserves better."

"I just point out his faults to improve him," Ludda-bee said. "If he weren't such a bumbling clod, he'd—"

"Ludda, no more about bumbling." She waited, but Johan-bee didn't speak. "My head hurts. How long did I lie there? I dreamed the Replica was found. Has it been?"

"I'm the thief."

"Master Uwald? You?"

"My Robbie despises me."

"I do despise you."

"Is the Replica back in place?"

Albin said, "We just found out it was Master Uwald."

Elodie said proudly, "Master Robbie proved it."

"Master Uwald, where is it?" the high brunka said.

"I won't say."

Master Tuomo shouted, "He wants to destroy the farm!"

"No, I don't."

"He wants people to die," Master Robbie said softly.

"I don't!"

Elodie frowned, believing him. Doesn't want to ruin the farm, although it will be ruined. Doesn't want to kill people, although people will be killed. Mmm. He doesn't care, really, about the people or the farm. What does he care about, other than Master Robbie? Ah. Lambs and calves! "You want one person to die, the one who won Nockess Farm."

He said nothing.

"He's there, the new owner?" Master Tuomo said. "You enticed him there?"

"With his death, no one would have known of the lost—"

"Hush!" High Brunka Marya put her hands flat on the table, palms down. "I feel Zertrum." She looked at Master Tuomo and Goodman Dror, the two whose homes were on Zertrum besides Master Uwald. "It's very bad." She blew her nose on her sleeve and wiped her eyes.

In the silence that followed, Elodie said, "Master Uwald, who was the other thief?"

"I acted alone." His eyes were on Master Robbie, always on him. "It was an ingenious plan. I placed the magic handkerchief in the Turtle Room. Then—"

"Did you close the door behind you?" Elodie asked. The disturbed rushes hadn't been mice!

"I left it ajar. Few come down that corridor. I waited there for Johan-bee to leave his post. When he did, I started the weeping and went into another room, which I also left ajar. I doubted Ursa-bee would notice, and she didn't. When she came, I ran into your chamber, Marya."

Elodie thought that a long dash for elderly Master Uwald.

He continued. "Later, after I had the Replica, I recovered the handkerchief."

Master Robbie said, "How did you know Johan-bee left?"

"I heard him. His steps are noisy."

"How did you learn where I hid the Replica?"

"How do you think, Marya? I purchased the information."

Elodie's mind veered off in a different direction. Her mastcress believed the Replica might not be in the Oase, where someone could stumble upon it. "High Brunka, is there a door from the Oase to the caves and tunnels of this mountain?"

"No, lamb." She turned back to Master Uwald. "From whom did you buy it?"

"I won't say. Son, I didn't mean . . ."

Elodie stirred her spoon absently in her bowl. If the Replica wasn't in the Oase or in the mountain, then it was outside. Master Uwald hadn't been out after the theft. He must have had help.

Who had gone out? Several bees had been to the stable to feed the animals, but the stable had been searched. A bee might have left the others and hidden the Replica in a tree hole, or might have dug a hurried hole for it, but that could be anywhere—not a useful line of thought. The high brunka said there was a cottage.

Without listening to what she might be interrupting, Elodie asked, "Has anyone searched the cottage?"

"Of course, lamb."

In her bowl, the brown stew and the yellow beans and the dark red beet juice made a muddy rainbow.

The beets!

Elodie—recklessly, rashly—announced, "I know where the Replica is." Unable to resist, she added, "I deduced and induced." Masteress, you'll be so proud of me. If you're alive.

Around the table, all heads turned to her.

"The Replica is where the beets were. Johan-bee buried it. He's the other thief."

Everyone looked at the door.

"He left!" Master Tuomo cried.

"No, I haven't."

With surprising stealth, Johan-bee had edged around the table, and now stood with his longbow raised, nocked, and aimed at the high brunka. At this near distance, he couldn't miss.

CHAPTER FIFTY-SEVEN

is breath coming in painful bursts, Count Jonty Um raced along the rim of the chasm, hoping to find a way off the mountain. The two people he'd dug out of the collapsed cottage managed to stay on his shoulder.

Below his thoughts, he felt animal terror, the fright of all the beasts he'd ever shape-shifted into. In the distance, through the roar of the fire, he heard voices crying out in despair and pain. He slowed. Fee fi! One voice sounded nasal, metallic, and not in pain. He stopped.

Couldn't be. Meenore wouldn't risk ITself to come here.

He heard the voice again. Singing! Fo fum! IT had, but where was IT in this confusion?

"Here—Meenore!" he roared. Running again, he continued to shout.

CHAPTER FIFTY-EIGHT

Elodie cursed herself for not thinking.

"Marya, I had to hit you with a bench before you'd help me." Johan-bee wasn't rocking, and his hands were steady on the longbow. "Master Uwald was always kind—the last time he was here, too. Master—"

"Anyone who is kind to you is the worst knave that ever lived." Ludda-bee's hands inched toward the nearest platter.

"Ludda, I will loose this arrow at you if you move again or say another word."

She stopped, her eyes bulging, her cheeks puffed out.

What to do? Elodie thought.

"Master Uwald," Johan-bee said, "please dig up the

Replica and saddle two horses. Please come back and tell me when you're ready."

"Excellent, Johan." Master Uwald took the bread knife. "I'll use it if I must. Robbie, come. Don't you want to be rich?"

"No, thank you. I want to be a barber-surgeon."

Master Uwald winced. He circled the table to Master Robbie's place and grabbed his elbow. "Come. You need someone who loves you."

Master Robbie, looking an appeal at all of them, went with him.

High Brunka Marya flicked her hand. A few inches of rainbow sprang from it and melted away instantly.

"Goodman Albin," Master Uwald said, "may I trouble you to open the door?"

Albin hesitated.

"Do it!" Ursa-bee cried. "He'll kill Marya."

Albin hauled open the big entry door. As he did so, Master Robbie broke free of Master Uwald's grip and bounded to the middle of the great hall.

"Robbie!" Master Uwald took a step toward him, then wheeled and left, into a night that was brightening toward dawn.

"Wherever you go, we'll find you," High Brunka Marya called after him. "You won't— Uh!" She shifted on her bench and gripped the table. "More tremors. Johan, you must—"

"Mistress Elodie and I"—Master Robbie spoke forcefully—"went to the room where the magic boxes were kept. . . ."

Why was he saying this? Elodie wondered. He was looking straight at her.

"We touched the *daffodil*." He almost shouted the word. "How we *laughed*."

What about it? No one was laughing now.

"I was *weak* with laughter. Then she— She's such a *mansioner*."

Lambs and calves! Despite her fear, Elodie pushed out a bubble of laughter. And another and another. Everyone smiled, even Johan-bee. She began to giggle. Albin joined in first, probably mansioning, too.

She stood, the better to laugh, and laughed harder, her laughter becoming real despite the tremors, the terrified people and beasts, her masteress, His Lordship.

Everyone laughed. Ursa-bee covered her mouth while laughing. Master Tuomo threw his head back. High Brunka Marya's shoulders shook. Master Robbie laughed while he nodded at Elodie.

Johan-bee's mouth opened wide with his laughter. He cried, "It's so funny. I helped steal the Replica."

Elodie hugged her belly, which ached from laughing.

Tears ran down her cheeks, tears of laughter and fear and sorrow.

Johan-bee's arms trembled with the force of his laughter. The longbow and arrow fell.

Master Tuomo, whooping with laughter, ran at him and toppled him. Albin snatched up the bow and arrow. Master Tuomo pulled the sword out of its sheath and pointed it at Johan-bee's chest.

With an effort, Elodie slowed her laughter.

Had Master Uwald already dug up the Replica?

Would he really come back for Johan-bee? She doubted it.

Ludda-bee took the sword from Master Tuomo. "Go catch Master Uwald. Johan won't get away from me. Will you, you great nincompoop?"

Two bees stayed with her, but everyone else who could surged toward the entry door, leaving the high brunka on her bench.

She cried, "I want to be there."

Elodie turned to see High Brunka Marya take an unsteady step. Mistress Sirka and Goodman Dror returned. Mistress Sirka scooped her up and carried her out, followed by Goodman Dror. The three of them and Elodie followed the others, who were disappearing down the stairs.

CHAPTER FIFTY-NINE

asteress Meenore drew breath to start ITs song again and heard His Lordship calling. From where? The tumult distorted sound, but a breeze momentarily tattered the smoke that blanketed Zertrum. IT saw His Lordship, running, one shoulder lower than the other, with two people clinging to that shoulder—running in the wrong direction, away from IT.

As IT chased His Lordship, IT devised a plan, though IT doubted there would be time. IT flew over them, turned, came down on a steep slope a few yards from the mouth of an enormous cave, probably newly made.

"Meenore! You came for me."

IT enjoyed for a sliver of a moment the humans' terrified faces. "Put your cargo on my back."

His Lordship nodded and reached for the two. He

glanced up the mountain. A river of molten rock flowed toward them as fast as gravy from a ewer.

No time to take the people and fly, IT thought. No time for His Lordship to shape-shift.

But they might reach the cave.

His Lordship saw, too, and sprinted toward it, still bearing the people. Masteress Meenore, who could only lumber on land, flapped ITs wings to give IT speed.

They reached the cave in time as the molten rock poured down. IT didn't mind the temperature, but IT couldn't fly through the flow. The people and His Lordship would soon die of the heat. Already their faces were red and strained.

Coursing up through ITs claws came Zertrum's rumble, this time far more powerful than anything that had gone before. The explosion was certainly moments away. Even a dragon couldn't survive that.

How strange, IT thought, accepting ITs fate, to die in this foreign place, attempting to save people and an ogre and becoming for eternity the good dragon. *Enh enh enh.*

CHAPTER SIXTY

ight was graying toward dawn. The flat land that led to the stable must have been the Oase vegetable garden before the blizzard. There Master Uwald was found, panting with effort as he dug. When he saw them, he waved the bread knife, but Master Tuomo ignored it and wrested the shovel away. Goodman Dror took the knife and held Master Uwald by his elbow.

"Careful!" High Brunka Marya clung to Mistress Sirka. "Don't damage the Replica, Master Tuomo."

Master Tuomo dug delicately but with haste, removing small quantities of dirt.

"There!" Ursa-bee breathed as a ruby appeared.

Master Tuomo dropped the shovel and continued with his hands. After a few minutes he unearthed the entire

Replica as well as the box that contained the handkerchief that wept.

How the gold and jewels shone despite the dirt!

Master Tuomo passed the Replica to High Brunka Marya, who held it against her chest. Ursa-bee took the box with the handkerchief. Everyone started back to the Oase, Mistress Sirka carrying the high brunka again and fairly leaping across the snow.

Would they be in time? Elodie wondered. The danger to Zertrum wouldn't be over until the Replica had been set back on its base.

Everyone rushed toward the Oase. Master Uwald was ushered along between Master Tuomo and Goodman Dror.

Elodie walked behind the rest with Master Robbie. Whenever Master Uwald looked longingly at him over his shoulder, Master Robbie turned and walked backward.

When they were almost at the entry, Master Robbie whispered, loud enough for only her (and the high brunka) to hear, "This is the beginning of better."

Lambs and calves, she admired him for that!

When they entered the great hall, High Brunka Marya was exiting into the corridor, supported by one of her bees and accompanied by three more, who, Elodie deduced, would stand guard over the Replica on its pedestal. Johan-bee lay on the floor with Ludda-bee looming over him and the sword point touching his chest. Another bee stood by in case he moved.

More bees took over to march him and Master Uwald out of the great hall. Elodie wondered where they'd be kept. As soon as they were gone, Ludda-bee dropped onto one of the benches at the table and wept noisily.

Deeter-bee sat, too, and took the last poppy-seed roll. "A historic event."

CHAPTER SIXTY-ONE

eenore!" His Lordship's voice rang in sudden silence.

The booming from below quieted. IT opened ITs eyes.

The flow of molten rock ceased. Outside the cave, the world turned the gray-white of drifting ash and new snow.

"Your Lordship, my Elodie deduced and induced and used her common sense and saved us both."

CHAPTER SIXTY-TWO

he fires in all three fireplaces had burned down to embers. Bees went to stir them up and add logs. Everyone else stood between the table and the door, waiting.

High Brunka Marya returned. Her serene brunka smile, absent since she'd discovered the theft, had been restored. "The tremors have stopped."

Elodie began, "Did the—"

Master Tuomo began, "Did the mountain—"

"I don't think the worst happened, but"—the smile faded—"there must have been a great deal of damage."

Ludda-bee burst out, "It isn't our fault, what Johan did. We all tried to improve him. I certainly did."

Elodie listened in astonishment.

Ludda-bee continued. "He isn't a bee anymore, is he?

He isn't worthy. He never was, really."

"He is a thief. The earl will decide if he's still a bee. We're to blame for making him suffer. He might not have listened to Master Uwald otherwise, but he's to blame for stealing." High Brunka Marya's voice was firm, but her smile remained. "I can't stop being happy."

Ludda-bee piled platters onto her tray. "I'm glad to have my kitchen to myself again." She marched out.

Albin asked the high brunka, "Did Johan-bee hit you on purpose?"

"I think he was just clumsy," Ursa-bee said.

Elodie's eyes met Master Robbie's. "I disagree," she said. "He and Master Uwald wanted to leave the Oase, which you"—she nodded at the high brunka—"were preventing. And they needed to talk without being overheard."

Master Tuomo said, "Uwald and Johan-bee are confined separately, aren't they?"

The high brunka said they were.

"In prison cells?" Master Robbie asked.

"We don't have any of those, pup. In rooms with two bees guarding each one."

"And they will be punished?" asked Master Tuomo.

"He did save your sons," Ursa-bee said. "Don't you pity him?"

Master Tuomo answered slowly, each word a blow. "I . . . do . . . not . . . pity . . . him."

"Lady El, how did they do it? We should make a play of it, but I don't understand."

Yes, they should. She could portray her masteress again. That would amuse IT—if IT was alive. She took a deep breath. "Johan-bee had the handkerchief that weeps. I expect that Master Uwald gave it to him. He told you"—Elodie nodded at Ursa-bee—"he was going to the garderobe, but he hurried to the Turtle Room instead. It was a long way, but he had time—"

"—because he always took so long. Grand— er, Master Uwald was waiting in the corridor outside the privy. He probably peeked and saw you leave your post."

Ursa-bee blushed. "I had to. The weeping was so piteous."

Elodie took up the tale. "Master Uwald ran into your chamber, High Brunka, and straight into the storage room."

"So that's where he was when Johan and I made sure the Replica was still there. Then Johan must have gotten the Replica from him before going out to dig up the beets. He said he needed the garderobe again."

Master Tuomo sat heavily on the bench by the table. "Master Robbie, girl, you did well."

Albin said, "Lady El . . ."

She shook her head. "I can't leave until I know what happened to my masteress." And His Lordship.

"But you can sleep. High Brunka? We can return to our rooms, right?"

"Oh, lamb! And pup! Yes. Go, everyone. It's morning, but no matter. Sleep!"

CHAPTER SIXTY-THREE

t the very moment the Replica was reset on its pedestal, the chasm closed on Zertrum and the volcano ceased spewing. The flow of molten rock that had already been released pooled and cooled quickly. New snowfall soon extinguished the fires that had broken out in myriad places.

But Zertrum didn't return to its previous state. Boulders that had moved stayed moved. Some farms that had been rich became sandy or too wet or too dry—or the reverse. Folks who'd been injured weren't miraculously cured. Worst of all by far, the seven people who'd been killed remained dead.

His Lordship and Masteress Meenore had to sleep and eat before flying back to the Oase. They slept the day through, then hunted—His Lordship as a wolf—and dined. By nightfall they were ready. The count raised his arms to shape-shift.

"Wait!"

His Lordship lowered his arms.

ITs white smoke spiraled upward. "I have deduced and induced that the villains are Master Uwald and Johan-bee and that the Replica was buried where and when the beets were harvested. At the Oase, I trust you will attest to this statement. I wish not to be accused of claiming brilliance only after the facts are widely known. If I was mistaken, so be it. I will accept the shame."

His Lordship nodded, shifted, and began to fly. IT rose, too, but IT couldn't match a swift's speed. The bird doubled back and circled the dragon to keep pace.

Upon waking, after sleeping around the clock, Elodie followed her rumbling stomach to the great hall. Before she went in, she heard coughing, and her heart rose to her throat. Inside, she found her masteress filling the entrance and His Lordship (dressed in his own clothes, taken from the stable) seated on a mound of mattresses that had been placed at the trestle table. Nesspa lay nearby, his eyes fixed on his master. As before, IT occupied the head of the table. The high brunka perched on her stool at the other end.

Bees and guests sat on the benches. Elodie raced across the great hall. She had hugged IT before so she didn't hesitate this time and stretched her arms across as much of ITs belly as she could reach. The corner of the table dug into her side. She inhaled deeply and licked her lips to fully take in ITs odor.

ITs white smoke curled in a spiral. "Mmm . . . Elodie . . . teeth and scales! If you must. Mmm . . . You were a credit to me. My confidence in you has been gratified."

Elodie! Credit to IT!

Finally, she stepped aside. "Zertrum didn't explode, did it?"

"No, Lodie."

She nodded, taking in the information. "When did you get here?"

"Perhaps half an hour ago. We deferred discussion of events on Zertrum until you joined us."

She felt a rush of gratitude.

IT turned to Master Robbie. "A portion of Elodie's credit belongs to you."

She was happy to share. "We solved the mystery together." She ran to His Lordship, who patted his mouth with the tablecloth, smiled his sweet smile at her, and stood, his head grazing the stone ceiling.

She wanted to hug him, too, but she never had, and he

was a count, so she contented herself with matching the ardor of his smile, if not its sweetness.

He sat again. "Would you like pottage?"

She nodded.

He ladled pottage into a bowl. A smiling Ludda-bee sat next to him, clearly reveling in his appetite. His own pottage filled a tureen. The others were seated, too, more tightly pressed together than usual.

"Why didn't you come right back to us?" Elodie said, addressing His Lordship. She took her bowl and squeezed onto the bench next to her masteress. "Did something happen?"

"Yes."

They all waited.

He put down his spoon. "When I was a swift, an arrow pierced my shoulder. As a bird, I couldn't fly." He resumed eating.

"So you had to get better." She paused for him to say more.

After the silence had stretched for half a minute, he said, "Meenore found me." He didn't mention the people he'd rescued.

"Your Lordship, if you please, relate the solution of the mystery as I revealed it to you on Zertrum."

Count Jonty Um obliged.

Master Robbie, sitting across from His Lordship, clapped his hands. "Whales and porpoises! IT knew."

Elodie suspected he wanted to be a barber-surgeon only because he couldn't be a dragon.

High Brunka Marya said, "Masteress, brunkas pay our debts. What is your fee?"

Elodie remembered that High Brunka Marya had promised a reward of a hundred silvers.

IT helped ITself from a platter of boiled eggs. "Madam, it is the quite reasonable sum of three gold coins."

Albin laughed.

Three gold coins equaled only seventy-five silvers. "But—"

"Lodie, do not tell me that I should be charit—"

"Masteress, there—"

"You have interrupted me, Master Robbie. I hope your reason is excellent."

He explained about the reward.

"I see." Blue smoke rose. "Nonetheless, I have named my price. I will not amend it."

High Brunka Marya opened her purse and produced the coins.

Albin asked, "How much of this will Elodie receive, Masteress?"

Elodie squeezed her hands together; she thought she deserved a portion.

ITs smoke tinted a delicate pink. "None. I pay her a salary."

The high brunka tucked her purse back under her cloak. "I'll go with you when you leave the Oase."

At gale speed, IT deduced her meaning. "You must not cease to be the high brunka."

Elodie blinked in surprise.

"I failed in the most important thing."

"You learned humility. The next high brunka will not have."

Elodie thought, IT has no humility!

"I'll think about what you say."

"There is a point upon which you can satisfy me," IT said. "It is my theory that you could not maintain your rainbow over the door for years or even weeks."

A rainbow fluttered out of High Brunka Marya's hand.

It was true! The high brunka was a mansioner, too!

IT pushed ITs bowl away. "I further contend that you made your claim to force the thieves to expose themselves, and the bumps on your head are proof of your success."

The high brunka's smile widened, but she didn't answer.

"I have eaten my fill, and now, Madam, I should like to see the Replica. Please bring the pedestal as well so there is no danger of a fresh disaster on Zertrum."

The high brunka left the great hall with four of her bees.

"Elodie, what do you deduce from this?"

She knew instantly and was shocked. "High Brunka Marya is willing for at least four bees to know where the Replica is hidden." How could she be careless again?

"Precisely."

While she was gone, His Lordship stood and stepped away from the table. Ludda-bee and another bee cleared the meal, and several other bees dismantled the table.

High Brunka Marya returned holding the Replica. The four bees carried the heavy marble pedestal between them.

"Unite the pedestal and the Replica, if you please."

They did.

"Ah. Beautiful," IT said, "and the workmanship is superb."

Elodie admired the Replica anew. The whole sculpture was no more than nine inches long, three or four inches wide, solid gold, curved as Lahnt was curved, spired with Lahnt's seven mountains in a line. The beauty lay not so much in the gold or even in the jewels that ran along the mountainous spine, but in the detail: the cliffs and crags marked with thin lines of rock fissures, the tiny evergreen forests, the specks of boulders.

"Masteress?" Elodie touched Zertrum on the Replica. "Do you think the real mountain is different now from the way it is here?"

"Mmm. It cannot—"

"Let me see, lamb." The high brunka leaned in close. "Bees and ants! The Replica is altered. The mouth of the volcano is flatter, and right here there used to be a forest." She pointed.

"What about the south slope?" Master Tuomo said, coming to stand next to her. "Can you see where Nockess was?"

"I can't tell, dear."

"Fascinating," IT said.

Bees and guests crowded close to see.

IT tapped a claw impatiently on ITs elbow. "Step away, if you please."

Only the high brunka hesitated.

"If you do not trust me now, Madam, you have learned nothing."

She backed away.

Flames flickered about ITs snout. IT aimed a jet of white fire at the base of the Replica.

Elodie deduced what IT was about: saving Lahnt forever.

"Is IT . . ." Master Robbie whispered in her ear.

She smiled at him. "I think so."

After a minute IT turned the pedestal while continuing to flame, until the fire had licked the base of the Replica all around.

Finally IT swallowed ITs flame. "High Brunka Marya, Lahnt no longer needs to hide the Replica, and you can never again be indiscreet about its location. It is now inseparable from its base. Zertrum is safe for perpetuity. You may thank me."

CHAPTER SIXTY-FOUR

he morning after His Lordship and Masteress Meenore returned to the Oase, they left again, along with Elodie, Albin, Nesspa (who would protect his master from the Potluck Farm cat), Master Tuomo, Mistress Sirka, and Goodman Dror. Mistress Sirka was going to help her beloved set up as a peddler, and they were to be wed.

The afternoon before they left, Goodman Dror explained his change of heart to High Brunka Marya in the great hall. Elodie hovered nearby to listen, in case she might someday mansion an excitable character who never knew her own mind and was easily influenced.

"I thought you loved being a bee," the high brunka said. "I'm sorry to lose you."

"You are?"

Mistress Sirka, standing at his side, prompted, "You didn't like it that High Brunka Marya could stop you from helping farmers. Bees have to listen to brunkas."

"That's right. Mistress Sirka says a peddler is his own master."

Elodie hid her smile. The husband of a barber-surgeon who dispensed love potions would not be his own master.

"And you adore me," she reminded him.

He nodded. "Yes, I do."

Perhaps it would go well. *She* adored *him*.

After this exchange, Master Robbie asked Elodie to help him shovel snow outside. Below the stairs, they began to clear a path from the stable to the cottage.

"Master Tuomo offered to be my guardian. He said a man can't have too many sons."

Really!

"But I'm staying at the Oase."

She was glad. He'd be safe, and he could give his affection freely to the bees he liked; he wouldn't be obliged to love any particular one.

"Whenever a barber-surgeon comes, I'll watch him or her. The high brunka says I'll have tasks, too. It will be like working at an inn, the way I used to help Grandmother." He plunged on. "We can start an inn together someday if detecting and barbering disappoint us."

Lambs and calves! What to say? Elodie threw snow to

the side to give herself time.

She didn't know if she'd ever see him again after they left the Oase. She liked him, too, but not enough to become an innkeeper.

What to say? She shoveled harder, her back to him.

She couldn't answer as herself or she'd stammer in confusion. Mansion a heroine who'd know what to do. Which one?

Penelope! A heroine who excelled at putting suitors off without discouraging them.

She stopped shoveling.

Now his back was to her.

"Master Robbie?"

He turned, his face red. "I didn't mean— You may not—"

"Hush." As Penelope, she had dignity and assurance. "Detecting and mansioning will always please me, but someday I may be in need of an original mind. Will you come?"

"Wherever you are, I'll come, by fast horse or quick cog."

"Thank you." Then, imagining Master Robbie as Odysseus, the hero of Penelope's tale, she leaned toward him and kissed his rosy cheek.

Master Tuomo chafed at the oxen's slow pace and remained with Elodie's party for only an hour before setting forth alone.

"Farewell." He bowed to all of them from his horse,

rode off, wheeled, and came back. "Before I go, Masteress, if you have charge of the girl, take my advice: Treat her as you would your steed. Rein her in, and do not let her have her head." He left them.

IT *enh enh enh*ed for several minutes. "As if I could do without your head, Lodie."

Goodman Dror and Mistress Sirka stayed with the oxcarts for three days, riding their donkeys as close as the beasts would go to ITs warmth. When they rounded the southern slope of Svye Mountain, however, they said their good-byes. The farm cottage of Mistress Sirka's parents, where the two would be wed, squatted in the valley below the road.

Two days later, the oxcarts reached the caves where the people of Zertrum had gone for safety, and where some still sheltered, planning to pass the winter before rebuilding their homes in the spring. Widow Fridda and her daughters were there, and each bestowed a hug on His Lordship. Other folks crowded around, patted his leg, tried to pump his hand. Elodie had never seen him look so happy—

—or Masteress Meenore so vexed. ITs smoke stayed a bright pink and ITs tail twitched the whole time, as people coughed, smiled, bowed, and waved. Luckily for them, ITs odor kept folks from coming close enough for conversation.

The remaining journey to Potluck Farm took a week, slower than it might have, because the road around

Zertrum was still obscured by haze and was blocked here and there by boulders that His Lordship and the oxen had to work together to remove.

Elodie spent the last day worrying. Would her father be able to conquer his fear of her friends? Would her mother try to wrench her away from them?

Albin and His Lordship shared her fear. His Lordship even offered to shape-shift into his monkey, although Elodie asked him not to. In midafternoon they reached the track that wound up the mountain to Potluck Farm, and Albin went ahead to prepare the way.

After an anxious two hours, as the sun was setting, he returned with Goodwife Bettel and Goodman Han, Elodie's mother and father, the faces of both bathed in joy. They'd heard reports of the good ogre and the good dragon, but even if they hadn't, they'd have welcomed any creatures who brought their daughter home. Albin made the introductions. Elodie's father bowed so deeply, his nose touched his knees.

His Lordship almost equaled the courtesy. In his opinion, Elodie's parents ranked with royalty. Nesspa performed a dog version of a bow, chest on the ground, rump in the air.

Masteress Meenore performed ITs elaborate bow and curtsy. "You are to be congratulated for producing a man-sioning and detecting prodigy."

Lambs and calves!

Despite her happiness, Goodwife Bettel merely crossed her arms. "If you value my daughter so highly, why did you leave her in danger at the Oase?"

Hastily, Albin—who had already told the story of the theft and of Elodie's connection with her masteress—suggested they continue talking at the Potluck cottage. The party began to ascend.

Elodie noticed ITs smoke rising in white spirals as they climbed.

Her father came to her side. "Is IT"—he lowered his voice to a whisper—"a *he* or a *she*?"

Enh enh enh. IT had heard.

"IT doesn't say."

The cottage could accommodate only an ogre's arm or a dragon's leg, so the humans brought a meal outside, and IT kept everyone warm. His Lordship sat on a tree stump with Nesspa at his feet while the humans perched on stools.

As she ladled pottage into bowls and a butter tub for His Lordship, Elodie's mother returned to her accusation. "Neither of you took good care of Lodie."

"Lodie?" Masteress Meenore's nasal voice rose in pitch. "You call her *Lodie*, too?"

Goodwife Bettel gaped at IT.

Elodie smiled.

IT collected ITself. "Life is risk, Madam, for children as

316

well as for adults. By being in danger, Lodie became more of what she can be. Why did you send her to Two Castles town?"

"To apprentice as a weaver."

"A weaver? Mmm."

Elodie hadn't confessed this to IT, since weaving had never been in her plan.

"You let her go because she showed no ability as a gooseherd. You let her go, although cogs have sunk in the strait and she had no one waiting for her and no preparation for the thieves of Two Castles, and she was, in fact, robbed on her first day."

Elodie's mother paled. Her father gasped. Albin sent Elodie a worried look. His Lordship grinned.

IT pressed on. "You sent her away because she wanted a different sort of life than she could have on a farm, because existence here has its own perils: blizzards, rockslides even without a volcano, drops over cliffs, floods, fires. You sent her away because you love her. And I took her in because—" IT broke off, perhaps surprised at where ITs rhetoric was leading. "Come, Madam, we both regard your daughter as precious. Let us be friends in this."

The contest ended. Goodwife Bettel busied herself with cutting bread for everyone. Elodie had never before seen her mother lose an argument.

"Elodie," IT said, "your parents have heard the broad

317

outline but not the particulars of discovering the thieves and the Replica."

This was an invitation to mansion. By firelight the two mansioners enacted events at the Oase and on Zertrum, Albin taking the male roles and Elodie the female. They did well and the applause was enthusiastic.

Elodie sat back down between her parents.

Goodman Han sighed. "It's a happy ending, but . . ."

"But it's very sad," her mother finished. "Master Uwald . . . Johan-bee . . . I don't want to feel sorry for them, but I do."

"Masteress?" Elodie said. "When there's a crime and you detect, when it's finished, is the ending ever truly happy?"

"Rarely."

Silence fell until IT said, "I do not relish a life lived out of doors. Your Lordship, when we reach Tair—"

"I'm not going to Tair."

"You're not?" Elodie cried.

"Nesspa and I will be bees on Zertrum for a while."

Dismayed, Elodie wondered if her masteress would stay on Lahnt, too. Would she have to herd geese again?

ITs smoke turned green—a confused dragon. "You will rusticate here, Your Lordship?"

"Wonderful!" Elodie's father put his arm around Elodie's shoulder.

Elodie flashed a look of appeal at her masteress.

Goodman Han continued happily. "Folks will need help, Your Lordship, and you can stay with us when you're not—"

"Nesspa and I will live better than most bees."

Meaning His Lordship didn't intend to live in the open outside a cottage. Elodie blushed for her friend's rudeness, which she knew he hadn't meant.

IT scratched ITs snout. "In the spring Elodie and I will continue on to Tair."

Phew! Elodie thought.

"Why?" Goodwife Bettel sounded ready to start another argument.

"I am a creature of town and city, of lair and hoard." ITs smoke spiraled. "I prefer the rub and chafe of people, fools though most of you be."

"Mother?" Elodie's father said, clearly hoping she would forbid their daughter to go.

But Goodwife Bettel accepted ITs decision. "Masteress, do you usually allow my daughter to be awake so late into the night?"

EPILOGUE

week after Elodie and her companions left the Oase, the earl of Lahnt arrived. High Brunka Marya pleaded for leniency for Johan-bee, taking on herself some of the blame for his part in the theft.

The earl, whose orchards on Zertrum had been ruined, condemned Master Uwald to spend the rest of his life in prison. Johan's sentence was ten years, and he was no longer a bee.

Master Tuomo visited his former master occasionally, perhaps out of gratitude for saving his sons. At first he gave Master Uwald a few coins so he might wager with the prison guards, but generosity became unnecessary, because Master Uwald had regained his luck, and he amassed considerable wealth in his confinement, which he put aside as an inheritance for Master Robbie.

Nockess Farm had taken the worst of the volcano: buildings collapsed, soil stony, flocks and herds scattered. Master Tuomo soon grew disgusted with the character of the new owner, Master Erick, and quit to purchase his own farm with his sons.

Master Robbie never visited Master Uwald. He finished out his childhood at the Oase. Deeter-bee taught him to read, and he devoured every book on healing. Even before he was fully grown, the high brunka ceased sending for a barber-surgeon when a bee was ill or afflicted with toothache. He wrote often to Elodie. She answered, and a correspondence flourished between them.

The Replica on its pedestal had pride of place in the center of the Oase's great hall. When guests came, Deeter-bee stood next to it, recounting the tale of its latest theft.

In the spring, Masteress Meenore and Elodie left Lahnt, after a tearful farewell that was made less sad by ITs promise to return regularly on the wing with Elodie, who was sure she had been granted the best of everything: frequent visits with her parents and Albin and the fascinating life of a detecting dragon's assistant.

In the northern harbor village of Dew they boarded the cog for Tair, where they planned to see the sights and where Elodie would proclaim, as she'd been hired to do:

"Today, in the kingdom of Tair and only in the kingdom of Tair, the Great, the Unfathomable, the Brilliant Meenore is available to solve riddles, find lost objects and lost people, and answer the unanswerable. Speak to IT with respect."